THE WORLD IN A NUTSHELL

Daniel Chase

PublishAmerica
Baltimore

Hardcover 978-1-4512-3697-2
Softcover 978-1-4512-3698-9
PUBLISHED BY PUBLISHAMERICA, LLLP
www.publishamerica.com
Baltimore

Printed in the United States of America

PART I

Leonard pulled his Honda hatchback into the courtyard where Lucille had told him to park. She had told him she'd leave the chain link gate open for him. He pulled the car up close to the entrance she'd described and killed the engine. He paused, took a deep breath and climbed out on legs that protested after being cramped in the car for the 1000 plus mile trip over from Michigan. He walked unsteadily back to the gate and closed it. There was no lock. No one was there to greet him, but this didn't surprise him much, as he told Lucille that he would probably get there around ten a.m. and it was only about 8:30. He had found the old mill town without difficulty, but the street signs seemed to be in hiding and he took several wrong streets before finding his way through the maze to the abandoned factory. Whoever dreamed up the name "Rustbelt" was right. Even the streets were rust colored. Everything seemed to be coated in an iodine-colored grit.

He sighed, wondering if he had made a mistake in coming here, but was slightly encouraged by the thought that in the past every decision he had questioned shortly after making it had always turned out for the best—maybe after rocky beginnings, but ultimately for the good. Yet he often had feelings of oppressive foreboding in the beginnings (and all along the way, his little voice that always insisted on honesty had to add). He felt that God provided the path, but God never promised it would always be on streets paved with gold. So, this was

Grover's Corner. It *seemed* like a corner—an out of the way corner of some out of the way state….

He looked around, hoping to be rescued from this feeling that he was a refugee that had just set foot on land after months at sea. But, alas, no.

He took a small overnight bag out of the car and climbed the steps to the person door off of a loading dock. He pushed the button by the door and heard nothing. He stood back a couple paces from the door, a habit he learned when he sold real estate one summer—if you stand close to the door, you scare the people who answer, step back and let them see all of you and you don't seem so overwhelming. He felt this might especially be true with him because he was now 6'-2" and weighed 230 pounds. Back when he sold real estate, in the late 70's, that was a pretty big person, but now it seemed every high school kid he saw was at least that big—even some of the girls.

Well, he had learned over his fifty-five years of life, if you want something to happen, take a piss. Seemed like any time he decided to do so while he waited for someone, that is when they would arrive. At the airport, they'd announce that your flight was boarding just as soon as you decided to go into the bathroom. If you were waiting for a ride somewhere and decided fifteen minutes after the appointed time that they would be late, and took the opportunity to take a leak, they would be waiting when you got out. Worked like a charm. He had remembered a spy series on TV once where one of the main characters told another that any opportunity you had you should either pee or sleep. Good advice, even if it was fiction on TV. Sleep would also be nice, he thought as he walked behind a squished and rusty car-sized box and urinated. He had just finished when he heard the door open behind him and turned to see Lucille standing on the loading dock, a ginger-colored cat in her arms. She had been known as "Cille" in college and he wondered if that was still the case. Seeing Cille's red hair, he had the scary thought that the rust had somehow imbued their very essences.

"Layo-nardo," Cille said, with a fake Italian accent, "Come on in!"

He picked up his bag and walked over to her. It had been a long time since he's seen her, recently only talking to her on the phone and through emails. She looked about the same as he remembered though and he wondered how he looked to her. "You've put on weight," she said. He looked down at his stomach and nodded in agreement. "It looks good on you," she added, "in college you were plain skinny!" He agreed with that too.

Her holding the cat precluded any hugging, so he gripped her shoulder with one hand and said, "It's good to see you again!"

"Good to see you too….Oh, this critter is Marm—short for marmalade, of course."

Leonard smiled at the cat and brushed it lightly with his closed hand, "Howya doin, Marm?" The cat wasn't sure she wanted to answer just then.

"I'll show you the place and then we can get you moved in. Want anything to eat or drink?"

"I'm okay."

"Yeah, you always were," she said. They walked past a small reception area and through a door down a short hall to what may have originally been a lunch room. She walked over to a cooler, an old-fashioned "ice chest" that was cooled with real ice and not hooked up to any electricity and took out a bottle of Coke. She opened it and handed it to him. "I assume you still drink soda?"

"Yeah, I do…" Leonard replied, patting his stomach. "Do you have any water too?" She had pulled a bottle of rum out of a cabinet and paused. "Well, that too," said Leonard, taking a good swig of the Coke and replacing the missing amount with rum." Cille showed him the bottled water dispenser with its five gallon jug. "Wow," he said, "Last time I saw one of these was on a mission trip to Mexico—only water safe for us Gringos to drink…." He took a paper cup and poured part of his rum and Coke into it and poured water back into the Coke bottle. "You may think it a bit odd, but straight Coke is too strong for me anymore…"

Cille laughed. "Nothing about you surprises me for more than a second or two…Haven't you noticed, or maybe someone told you, but you, and I, are not your typical Americans? We're not even your typical *people*."

"Yeah, I have been sort of rudely introduced to that concept, on several occasions."

"Uh huh…." She put the cat down and they continued the tour, Leonard leaving his bag in the lunch room.

"I can pick that up later, don't let me forget…been doing a lot of that recently, but only the important things."

Cille put the cat on the floor in the hallway and they walked along the hallway, Cille pointing out various small, empty offices as they went. Some had dusty desks and other office furniture, still looking much the way they did before the factory closed, in the early 80's, Leonard guessed, though from the furnishings, it could have been in the 30's or 40's.

"We haven't done a thing with the offices, or much anywhere on the ground floor or the floor below." Cille ushered him past an elevator to a stairs. "If we had more electricity, we could run the elevators, but why bother? It's been so long, we couldn't even be sure they're safe."

"Well, if you decide to move more equipment in, or even more people, it would be nice to at least get the freight elevators running again. I know they're supposed to have inspections, but don't recall just how often. We'd have to get an engineer or at least an inspector to determine if they're safe to operate. Not having been run in ages probably hasn't helped them, although it means there's been less wear and tear on the equipment," Leonard said.

After sitting in a car for hours on end, Leonard's legs felt a bit rubbery on the stairs, but it felt good too to be moving.

Cille said, "Let's go up to the roof and work our way down—that way you can get a sort of overview."

Once he got going, Leonard's legs felt better and he followed Cille up the steps. She still had a nice rear end and muscular legs, and the shorts she was wearing showed them off. Thus distracted, he was less aware of the number of steps, though he had "counted," as was his custom (he counted steps he took when he went for a walk, or mowed his lawn—in fact he counted lots of things, though not always in any rational order (often starting over at "one" at least once during the counting)). He counted pretty much in order this time and had counted landings to, so when he started on "six-one," he figured he had fourteen more steps till seven and thought they must be getting near the top by now.

He remembered that as a county planner who took over as a manager of a Federal "HUD" project for which he had been the lead planner, he could run up five flights of stairs with little difficulty—but he had been about 30 years old at the time. Back then, he drank more heavily, smoked reefer, and had just started doing tai chi, so all in all, he was probably in better shape now. Nonetheless, he was glad when they reached seven and she led him to another, smaller, iron-grated stairs that after seven steps and through a door they were on the roof.

The bright sunlight was dazzling after being inside. He followed her silhouette across the gravel and around the elevator penthouse. She stopped and by that time his eyes had adjusted and he looked out over the small industrial area, maybe a quarter mile square, with railroad tracks along side the building defining one edge. He followed her to another wall and saw the largest part of the town laid out like it was on a sheet of plywood for an HO scale train set in someone's basement, with a brownish river which had a railroad line and a highway beside it that divided the town almost into two equal sized parts, each one maybe a mile by two miles. The river had several picturesque rust colored bridges over it. The vantage point wasn't high enough to see any neighboring towns. The third side showed mostly ribbons of water and woods. The forth side was hills—what he would have called mountains in Michigan.

He was reluctant to leave the roof, as he looked over the sleepy little town and sipped his drink.

"I'd point out things, but right now it probably wouldn't make a lot of sense to you; we can come back up here in a couple days to sort of put it all together." Cille touched his arm and, reluctantly he let himself be led back into the building. On the way, he noticed some plantings and water tanks and asked about them.

"Oh, I'm glad you asked. Those are a couple of our infant projects. We have a produce garden, mostly salad vegetables and some herbs and some water storage tanks for use in the building, and for the garden. We want to start a hydroponic garden and a solar water heater for washing and so on, and we want to do something with reclaimed water and sewage."

"Sounds ambitious."

"I thought it would be something you'd be able to help with."

"Yeah, I would like to. If those are the hot water tanks, I'd move them closer to the penthouse wall and paint it silver and them black, maybe insulate, put a covering over...." He started thinking how he could move them, what the support structure was. "I'd need to see the roof structure—do you have blueprints?"

"Later...hold your horses, chief. Let's do first things first!"

"By the way," Leonard said as they turned away, "you are aware that one of the herbs you are growing there looks to be marijuana?"

She gave him a little surprised look and led him back inside and down the stairs. Before the outer door closed and they were back in twilight, he noticed that her hair was thinning and graying (at least she wasn't dyeing it, he thought). He felt his way down the first stairs to the seventh floor.

She stopped at the bottom of the iron stairs and waved her hand in a big arc. "This is where we live."

Leonard looked around the huge expanse of floor, about twice the size of a basketball court, punctuated by brick columns. It was fairly well lit—having a wall to ceiling expanse of windows on every wall. Many had been boarded up or covered in some way, but the entire wall on what he guessed to be the south wall, was all pristine windows. They were dirty and some were cracked and patched, but it was all glass and lit the space quite well. The ceiling, divided into handball court sized portions by steel trusses sitting on the columns, was at least 20 feet from the concrete floor. Someone had put up partitions on the floor between columns to divide portions of the space. The partitions were only 6 to 8 feet tall.

"So, we all live on this one floor?" he said, not daring to believe that by "we" she had only meant "he and she." He remembered Lucille talking about other people living there, but wasn't exactly sure how many it was.

"Oh, no, I mean Robert and me."

Leonard felt deflated, he didn't think that "Robert" was the name of a cat--he knew she had about two dozen cats.

"Oh, speak of the devil, here he comes now!"

Leonard was prepared to hate him, but when I man who looked like Abe Lincoln rode up on a Segway scooter, he couldn't find any hate for him. He had known Cille for a long time and knew her eccentric character would be hard to match, but it appeared instantly that she had succeeded in finding her soul mate. Robert had a big black and gray striped cat draped on his shoulders. He stopped in front of them, nodded and touched the brim of his stovepipe hat and gingerly offered a huge hand to Leonard. "You must be Leonardo—so glad to make your acquaintance. Sorry for my namby-pamby handshake, I'm still getting used to this scooter and if I shift my balance by accident, I find myself flying off in a new direction that I hadn't planned on!"

Leonard laughed in spite of himself. How could he feel malice towards such a delightful man? "Well, Robert, it's a pleasure to meet you too."

"Oh, call me Abe, everyone does! I'm not really Abraham Lincoln though." In a stage whisper, behind his hand as if talking to a co-conspirator, he added, "That would be just plain crazy!...I just admire him and like to dress like him." He zoomed off, as if being dragged by a horse with a will of its own, calling over his shoulder, "Well, nice meeting you, perhaps we can have lunch…."

"So," Leonard said, turning back to Cille, that's your live-in boyfriend…."

"Yes; Robert—Abe. I hope you aren't upset…I didn't know how to tell you and I guess I feared that you wouldn't come if I did…." She trailed off, turning to watch Abe as he tooled around the floor on his Segway. "And, we were sort of seeing each other, but we didn't actually move in together until a couple weeks ago."

Leonard was still trying to process it all, knowing that he and Cille had never been a real match, had always struggled to maintain a friendship, flirting with a closer relationship, but never being able to make it work for more than a few moments at a time. It seemed they had always been emotionally closer when they were geographically distant.

Cille showed Leonard around their quarters—they had made partitions out of plywood; some were painted and some had cloth stretched across the inside surfaces. Some partitions seemed to be just frames covered with light, translucent cloth. He assumed that was to make the most of sunlight, since the only light came from the outer walls of windows. In one area that he guessed was the bedroom, they had boxes and crates piled up as walls.

Cille led him down the stairs to the sixth floor. She told him this was where Boris and Natasha lived at one end and Tom and Liv stayed at the other. She explained that Boris and Natasha were really Boris and Theomina, but everyone just called her Natasha. Boris was a retired engineer and Natasha did "Energy work." Leonard asked if she were in the nuclear power industry and Cille replied, "Oh, goodness no, she does Rieke and acupressure massage—you know, energy work."

"Oh, yeah, Reike—like working with Orgone Energy, or 'chi' or 'prana.' Gotcha."

He wondered if there were a hierarchy of position in the building based on rank in the "organization" with the higher ups getting the higher floors and more room, and by the time they got to the basement there would be a warren containing five hundred hunchback troll sewer cleaners—with a small cubbyhole for Leonard too.

On fifth floor Cille dispelled his negative thinking by announcing, "And here is where we thought you might like to stay." The room was empty and dusty and the same size as the other two he had seen. "This is the last of the smaller floors, and because of that, it has access to the roof of the part of the building below it. Right now it is just windows, but you could easily put a door in."

She looked at Leonard's face and said, "If you don't like it, we can find something else—there are four other floors plus the basement. Some others have already staked out spaces, but things could be re-arranged if necessary..."

"No, this is fine—more than fine—it's just so overwhelmingly big! I don't need anywhere near this amount of space!"

13

"Well, we thought with your art you would like studio space, and then you could have a place to do experiments and stuff, and, you'll love this; there is a little alcove where you could write!" She walked across to on wall and he saw that there was a sort of turret. He followed her over. It was small, but he immediately liked the space—it seemed right somehow—cozy but with windows so he could look out onto the courtyard where his car was parked.

"And, of course, with all the windows there is north light"— she swept her hand towards what must be north, and then they walked in the other direction towards a bank of windows at one narrow end. They did indeed look out on a roof—the roof was about two-thirds the size of the floor he was on.

"Well, this certainly is nice and it suits me. I just feel I'd be taking up space that others may want."

Cille replied, "Well, like I said, there are four other floors for people to choose from and maybe later we can rearrange and people can share more. Right now there are only four couples, another single guy and you. Later we hope to get maybe 40 people living here. Enough to be close while still allowing some anonymity. We want people to feel that they are independent and free, not being observed by their neighbors, like what sometimes seems to happen in small towns, but few enough that there is still a feeling of solidarity and neighborliness."

"Sounds like someone has thought about this pretty hard!" Leonard said. "Reminds me of a commune, but without the baggage…" The last he said with a little doubt creeping into his voice.

"Right. We wanted the best part of communal living, but yet more independence—more like living in an apartment or condo, but with a little more feeling of community. More like a co-op."

In his younger days, when he was working as a community planner, Leonard had thought about communal type living and had come to the conclusion that a co-op would be about the best way of doing it. He even thought of making it a corporation with each "shareholder" being a tenant and each "share" being the physical holding—the actual apartment or living space.

"I must say that Robert came up with most of the ideas for the structure of the place and its governance…"

"Big surprise there…!" said Leonard.

"What?"

"Nothing. So, tell me more."

"Oh, I get it, Abe Lincoln—governance. Well, there's not much more to tell; you can talk to Robert more about the government and so on. Right now you can stay as a guest and see what you think—no commitment. But if you decide to stay, there would be a more formal arrangement…."

"Is there rent or a mortgage or something like that—right now I am a little low…"

"Well, in that sense, we are more like a commune—you donate whatever you can…"

"'From each according to his abilities...' sort of thing?"

"Exactly. And in return you have housing and some food—mostly from the garden at this point, but we are trying to get status to run a soup kitchen and then..."

"Like in the book *Ringolevio*..." He saw her blank look. "It has actually been done before by a group in New York City—but they weren't 'official,' if I remember correctly. They went around and collected donations of food leftover from restaurants and ran a soup kitchen and also had enough for themselves."

"Well, that's it. That's what we are hoping to do. What was the name of the book?"

"*Ringolevio.* Not sure of the spelling and forgot who wrote it. Be nice to have a copy. I think I used to own one, but almost all my books were destroyed in the fire." He blinked the flood of emotion away and looked out the window.

"What if I like it here, but you all don't think that I am 'a fit' (to use the modern term)?" he said after a minute.

"That hasn't happened so far, but like I said, we only have a half dozen so far. That's something we're working on and we are going slowly with inviting people at this point for that very reason. We don't want to end up like a snooty 'gated community' with lots of rules and regulations and keeping the riff raff out..."

"Hell, some of my best friends are riff raff—I'm riff raff!" Leonard said.

"Exactly," said Cille and Leonard wasn't sure how to take that, but she added, "In someone's eyes there is always someone else who is viewed as an undesirable. But, we often find that the people we would not choose as friends, or whom we choose not to associate with, are indispensable to a society."

"Absolutely."

"Well, you can start moving in here—generally we were thinking of the new people—guests—moving into the offices on ground floor to start with. That's what Morrie did. That way if they move out again it is easier, but since those places aren't really ready and I just have a good feeling about you, we felt that this would be good for you…I mean, if it's okay with you!" She added hastily.

"Yeah, it's fine. I don't have that much to move in anyway. Maybe we can get the freight elevator running by the time I scrounge up more stuff."

"I'll show you the rest of it on the way down. And we can find whatever you need to set your place up and meet everyone else." She turned and started back down the stairs.

Leonard followed and looked one more time at his new digs before going down the stairs.

Cille called over her shoulder, "The fourth floor seemed to be the gathering point of junk and spare parts and so on, so it is vacant and needs probably the most work before it can be used"—she waved at the door as she passed it on the landing and continued down the stairs. Leonard paused and opened the door enough to look in—she was right; it was a mess. Something bothered him more than that, but he was drawn away by Cille continuing the tour and he hurried to catch up to her.

"Right now Richard and Jill live on third floor…lest you be confused, Jill is short for 'Gillian' and Richard and Jill are both guys and are 'partners.'" She stopped and gave Leonard a searching look before opening the door to the third floor.

Leonard knew she wanted a response and he said, "Whatever floats your boat." He felt he should add more, so he continued, "I believe in God and I believe in Jesus Christ, but I have trouble with the idea that God created people who from birth, apparently, have a predilection to have sex with people of the same gender and then decided to condemn them for it. Some people are even born with the 'wrong' external genitalia, or both sets of gonads, so how can God condemn these people? At any rate, I am not going to condemn them or even criticize them. One more thing—my stepdaughter Ariel always thought I hated gays and lesbians. When our church voted whether to accept an openly lesbian pastor, we had to vote on it and there were two votes against her. Riding home in the car, I said I was glad that the pastor was accepted and Ariel said, 'Really, I thought one of those two votes was yours!'

"I told Ariel that indeed neither of those votes was mine and that in fact when the Council had discussed the matter, I, (being a member of council by virtue of being the chairman of the Board of Trustees), spoke in favor of offering the woman the job as pastor when another man said that he personally had nothing against a lesbian pastor, but felt we should not offer her the job because others in the church might have a problem with it. I told him, and the rest, that first of all, we needed to stop anticipating what other people might think or say or do and start speaking for ourselves and secondly, that right is right and I moved that we vote to offer the position to the woman."

Leonard took a deep breath. "Later, when Ariel went to college, she took *Women's Studies* and hung around with lots of gays and lesbians. When she was home on break one summer, I asked her if she were lesbian and she got mad and wouldn't talk to me for several days. The whole thing gets rather confusing."

Cille pushed the door open.

By the time they finished their short tour, there were three of the couples and Abe in the lunch room, along with an old, brown guy on the couch who looked like he either had just awakened or was just going to sleep. Abe motioned Leonard and Cille to sit with them at a table.

"I just thought it would be nice to welcome you to our humble abode and make more formal introductions and just give us all a chance to get to know each other a little," Abe began. "Oh, Richard Corey and Jill Baker will join us for lunch, but had a previous engagement. I can only imagine how intimidating it is for you, Leonardo, to suddenly find yourself thrust into a group of relative strangers. Cille, of course has talked to you about us, but that isn't the same as meeting and then living with people. Any of you who have been married know what I mean!"

Leonard found himself wondering if that meant Abe or any of the rest had been married in the past and if any were married now. He also wondered about Richard Corey's name.

"First, introductions…" Abe continued. "You have heard about Leonardo from Cille and me, so I will just introduce you to him and then let Leonardo say anything he wants. Leonardo, to your immediate left is Boris Medelius." Boris was a small, muscular, wiry guy with a Marine-style crew cut—an almost shaved head of blond hair and penetrating blue eyes. He reminded Leonard of a gymnast. He nodded towards Leonard. Leonard made a mental note, *Boris the gymnast*.

"Next to Boris is his wife, whom we affectionately call 'Natasha'." She turned and smiled at him, showing a little of an overbite. She too was small, but not muscular, having an almost voluptuous figure and a dark, Gypsy-like look about her, accentuated by violet and red-violet clothing accessorized with scarves. Her hair, dark, almost black but with highlights of purple, was tied up with a paisley scarf in tones of umber, purple and gold. No need to make a mental note to help Leonard remember her name.

Abe continued the introductions, "Next are the floor-mates of Boris and Natasha, Tom and Liv."

Tom was heavy set, dull and nervous. Mental note—*Tom Smothers*. Tom glanced up at Leonard from under thick eyebrows and murmured something Leonard didn't hear. Liv had bleached blond hair in a brushy ponytail that stood up like a topknot from the middle of her head. Leonard thought of Cindy Lou Who from the Doctor Seuss book. She was frail with big, innocent eyes. He noted, *Liv in Whoville*. She smiled shyly at him.

Abe continued, "Oh, and over on the couch is Morrie." Leonard hated to judge, but since the pudgy man was dressed in a rumpled brown suit, his mental note was, *Morrie the couch potato*. Abe added, "We'll make further introductions at lunch, when Richard and Jill arrive. Is there anything you'd like to say by way of introduction—maybe where you are from, what you do, your favorite opera...."

Leonard glanced up, not sure if he heard right, or if Abe was serious. Seeing no reaction, he replied, "Sure. Thanks Abe. It is nice to be here. I am from Michigan." He held up his hand, thinking Abe would get a kick out of it, and as he pointed to the web of his thumb added, "Right here." Getting blank stares from most and a knowing smile from Abe and Cille, he almost stopped to explain that the lower peninsula of Michigan is hand-shaped and people there have a habit of using the palm side of their right hands as maps when they tell people where they live, but decided to remain "mysterious." He continued, "My wife left me just after the house burned down and went to live with one of her daughters. I was an artist and almost all of my work was destroyed. I did save some novels I'd written. My father was my only tie to Michigan really, and he died just before the fire." He blinked and swallowed and went on quickly...

"I had been corresponding with Cille; she and I met in college at Western Michigan in Kalamazoo, Michigan. (He resisted the urge to show them where that was located on his hand-map.) "When she offered to let me move in here, I thought, 'Why not?'"

Realizing that this probably didn't sound very complimentary to them, and noticing some look up sharply, he gave them a quick smile to let them know it was sort of a joke, but sort of not. He wasn't very good at this sort of thing. He shrugged. "That's about it. Oh, my favorite opera is Wagner's Ring Cycle, although I must say I'm not much of an opera maven." He looked around nervously. "I guess I'm still in shock and am afraid if I talk much I will break down." Even he was surprised that he said this and ducked his head, not daring to look at anyone.

He felt someone patting his hand and looked up to see Natasha crouched beside him so her face was even with his. She looked into his eyes. "I see much pain. *Mnoga bolyen.* You understand these words, I see. It will pass…" She patted his hand once more and stood up. He wasn't sure he had heard her right, but felt better somehow.

"Well," Leonard said as he jumped up. "I guess I should get my stuff out of the car."

Everyone but Morrie, who had allowed gravity to win and was lying down again, followed him out—he was surprised when each held out his or her arms for a load of his possessions to take upstairs. Cille opened doors for the parade of movers and he thought suddenly that she was the janitor (not in the American sense of a person who cleans, but in the British sense that she was the gate keeper, the custodian; janitors being named after Janus, the Roman god of gates). They all put their loads down by the door from the stairs and drifted off. He and Abe made two more trips.

On the last trip, Richard and Jill showed up and each offered to take an armload. Leonard looked at the tall, dark haired, handsome man and said, "Richard…" and offered his hand.

The man stepped back and said, "I'm not Richard..." then seeing Leonard's reaction laughed and shook his hand.

The thin redhead next to him slapped the dark-haired guy's shoulder and said, "Oh, you!" Then turning to Leonard said, "He always does that! He thinks it's immensely humorous, silly, Foo Foo! I am *Jill* and he *is* Richard." The redhead was stunning; he had delicate features, a sort of pixie hairdo and incredibly beautiful green eyes.

Inadvertently, Leonard whispered, "Wow!" Then stepped back and murmured an apology.

"Oh, no need. We are used to it, aren't we, Killer?" Jill punched Richard playfully. "Killer's not the jealous type! Thank God for *that*!"

"Amen," Leonard said. Suddenly he remembered the time he was at a Halloween dance, dancing with his friend's girlfriend when a man dressed as a woman tapped him on the shoulder to cut in and he impulsively said, "Well, okay..." and then grabbed the guy and waltzed around the floor with him. Made him the hit of the party. He had not dressed in costume, but kept his trenchcoat on and had flipped up the collar so he was 'the spy.' Another image from that party suddenly intruded—skeletal death in the hooded robe standing in the corner with his scythe. Leonard had never been sure if that had been another party-goer in costume, or....

They took the last of his things upstairs and he saw that someone had but a bed frame and mattress by the pile of his things. They went downstairs to the lunch room. On the way he chatted with Abe and Richard and Jill about how nice it would be to have an elevator working. He thought maybe they could rig up a sort of dumb waiter that could just be pulled up by hand through the elevator shaft until something better could be rigged. He said he had noticed how windy it was up on the roof and perhaps they could somehow have a wind mill to power things—even an elevator.

Jill started joking about, "Oh, sorry, darling, can't use the elevator today, the wind isn't blowing." Every time Jill spoke, Leonard had to look again and remind himself that this was a *man* and he should not be the least bit attracted.

Abe told Leonard that today was special, normally they tried to have dinner together, and whoever was around often sat together for other meals, but since they all knew he would be arriving today just before noon, they thought it would be nice to have a lunch with everyone together. Leonard said he appreciated the gesture.

Abe asked Boris to return thanks and then the sat down to a lunch that consisted of a big salad of fresh produce and a loaf of crusty bread, some cheese and yogurt. A jug of red wine and a jug of apple cider circulated freely and Leonard had some of each and thought they were very good. When he commented, he was told that Jill and Richard had pressed apples to make the cider and had also made the wine.

"The cider is a bit young yet; I like it when it has just started to go hard," Jill said and Richard replied, "You would." That got a laugh from most of the group.

When they had finished lunch, people got up from the table and each made it a point to welcome Leonard to their group. He felt very good. Abe told him that they more or less spent their days with everyone doing their own thing, but, as he had mentioned, they would get together again for dinner and after dinner they would have a more formal meeting to discuss things. He said they needed more structure if they expected to accomplish anything with getting the building more in order. Leonard agreed.

Seeing a potential ally, Abe said, "Right. While I think a government that governs best governs least, I still think at least in the beginning we need to have more structure and even assign work groups to certain tasks. We need to draw up a list of tasks and put them in order of priority. We need to get volunteers, if possible, to head up each crew and get important things done. We may even need to enlist outside workers to help—don't know how that would work, since we are hardly an official organization…"

"Talk to churches and maybe shelters—may be able to find volunteers in those places." Leonard said.

"Good. Good….Well, before we run off with too many ideas and so on, you may like to freshen up. In the summer we have rigged up a shower on the upper roof and it should be warmish, or you might find it more to your liking later in the early evening, since it is heated by the sun."

"Yeah, I can wait on that, if you can stand my smell…"

"Young man, I have worked on a farm, so I doubt that you can compete with some of the smells I've had the pleasure of enjoying."

"I do think I would like to take a nap. Didn't sleep well on the road and the drive has tired me out."

Abe smiled, "Sure. You saw the bed upstairs, should be easy enough to put together. I see you do not have a watch, but we will meet back here for dinner around six. I can send someone up to your place…"

"Oh, I usually wake up at the time I set in my mind, and I doubt that I would sleep for more than an hour, but if I am not here by six, that would be nice, just this one time."

"Yes, it would be…no wake up calls in this hotel!" Abe said so heartily that Leonard couldn't take offense.

"See you around six then," Leonard said as he left the lunchroom.

Leonard got his tools from the pile of his belongings and set up the bed. He picked the Northwest corner, furthest away from the stairwell. *This may not be good in the event of a fire,* he though and he wondered about bathroom facilities, having seen none and knowing there was no running water. The thought reminded him that his bladder was full, so he decided to walk down to the courtyard and maybe encounter someone to ask along the way. He also wanted to see about scavenging some materials for his "apartment" from the stuff on fourth floor or elsewhere.

As he passed fourth floor, he thought maybe as long as he was there, he would see what there was that he might use. He turned back and opened the door. Immediately he smelled smoke. Maybe just a must odor or something, but he decided to check it out. He saw a reddish glow by the elevator and went over. A pile of rags was smoldering there. He looked around for a fire extinguisher in the semi-darkness. He soon gave up. Nearby he did see a fifty-five gallon drum that had the top cut off and probably had been used as a waste can. He brought it over, tipped it upside down over the rags. He checked that nothing else was on fire and ran down to third floor. He pounded on the door and threw it open and shouted "Fire!" Hearing no response, he went down to ground floor and found Abe and Cille.

"There's a fire on fourth floor!" He said, breathlessly. They looked alarmed and ran toward him. "I think I contained it, but we'd better check—are there fire extinguishers?"
Abe grabbed one from the cabinet on the wall and the three of them ran up to fourth floor. Leonard flipped the can over and before Abe could spray the extinguisher he stopped him and kicked the rags into the can again and upended it. "Now they won't fly around when you spray." Abe hosed them down and they carried the drum down the stairs and outside.

Leonard excused himself and ran behind the metal box he'd used before and relieved himself. Coming back he said, "Pardon me, but all the excitement…."

"No problem…" said Abe. "Actually it is a problem. Most of us have been urinating into the floor drains, though not always so convenient. With the other, we have an arrangement in the courtyard in the corner and another up on the top roof. But that might be a priority." He interrupted himself, "But, tell me about this fire—how did you discover it? How do you think it happened?"

"Looks like spontaneous combustion. Oily rags will ignite by themselves—but why now?—if they had been there since this place shut down, something would have happened long before this. I was going down to answer the call of nature and I smelled smoke and found the fire. Just lucky I had to go and didn't take a nap first!" He thought for a minute about why they would start on fire now. "Do you have any enemies—someone that doesn't want you here?"

Abe laughed. "Well, very few people even know that we are here, and perhaps some of them are not keen on our being here, but I can't see them trying to burn us out. That's pretty extreme! There must be some other logical explanation."

They went back inside and sat down in some comfortable chairs in the lunch room where Morrie was still asleep on the couch. They continued to talk. Cille had made tea and they all were drinking it when Boris and Natasha and Tom and Liv came in. Abe told them about the fire. They were all surprised. Leonard found his paranoid-self kicking in and observed them closely to see if any of them could have intentionally set the fire.

They seemed genuinely surprised and disconcerted. Leonard's thoughts were interrupted by Richard and Jill slamming into the room. But they were just being their usual katzenjammer selves and were taken aback when everyone looked at them. "Whaaat?" said Jill.

Abe said, "We were just discussing an incident that occurred a short time ago—a fire on fourth floor. You wouldn't know anything about it, would you?" He saw their response,

"Let me rephrase that—Have you been on fourth floor and could you have unintentionally started a fire?"

"No!" They both chorused.

But Leonard's paranoia found fuel when Richard looked at him and said, "Odd that this would happen the very day that you arrive and that you are the one who discovered it....Didn't you say you had a fire back in Michigan?"

Leonard didn't like the direction this had taken and his heart started pounding. He jumped to his feet, but was unsure what to do next, other than act on the urge to beat Richard to a pulp. Abe held up his hand and stepped in front of Leonard, "Now, now..." and turning to Richard said, "I also take umbrage at your insinuation. What in the blue blazes would make you suggest..."

"Well," Jill suddenly interjected, "I was on fourth floor, but did nothing that would start a fire. Let's see, when was it? You remember, Richard, it was the day I refinished the floor and..."

Leonard interrupted, "Refinished—did you use something like boiled linseed oil?"

"Yes, as a matter of fact, I did, I did use BLO." He giggled.

"And when you finished, what did you do with the rags?"

"Oh, cripes, I don't remember. Put them somewhere, threw them away, I'm sure. Who cares about some used rags—I can get more if you need them, good grief..."

Leonard interjected, "Do you know that oily rags can start on fire by themselves? They just generate enough heat that they start to burn if you leave them in a pile?"

"Really?" Then it dawned on Jill what the concern was, "Oh, my, no, I didn't know. I may have left them up there—I was in a hurry to get to dance class and I may have just left them to pick up later. Oh, my God!"

"No problem," Leonard said, "Now you know, so it won't happen again." He sat down, not even wanting to look at Richard. Then he stood back up and left the room and went out and sat on the fender of his car. He felt drained, wasn't sure if he wanted to cry or vomit. What had he done? Why had he ever come here? He thought about getting into the car and driving back home. But where would that be? He was homeless and had no friends. He looked up at the sky and sighed, "Oh, God, help me…" He felt a hand on his shoulder. He didn't even look to see who it was. "I'm sorry," he said to the unknown presence, "if there were a bridge here, I'd be on the railing…"

He was surprised that the voice was not Abe's or even Cille's; it was Natasha who said, "Don't talk like that…remove such thoughts from your mind."

"I don't know what to do! I feel…torn into a hundred pieces, I feel like trash blown by the wind, I don't think I can…" He found himself sobbing. He hid his face in his hands. He hated for her to see him that way.

He heard the door open and Cille call to them as he hurriedly brushed the tears from his face. "I've made some chamomile tea; why don't you both come in and have some with us?"

He turned to Natasha and mumbled, "Yeah, chamomile tea'll fix everything!"

She smile and squeezed his hand, "You may be surprised."

"I doubt it, but…"

"What did I tell you?" she said sternly, "You must, for your own health, banish such thoughts."

He stood up, "Thank you…I'm sorry…."

"Nothing to be sorry about. Now let us go have tea."

He wiped his face on his sleeve and followed her into the lunchroom.

The others were sitting around the table and Cille got up and poured two new cups of tea and sat down again. Abe stood and turned to welcome Leonard. "Let's do this again. Welcome Leonard! I welcome you to this place and bless your presence. I banish any shades and shadows that may have followed you here." Abe turned from Leonard to look upon the group and said, "Leonardo is our guest and under my aegis." He embraced Leonard, nearly knocking the breath from him. Abe turned him toward the group and holding him at his side with his arm around Leonard's shoulder.

One by one, the group stood and came over and shook his hand or embraced him. Last was Richard, who said, "I was out of line. I'm sorry."

Leonard looked him in the eye and said, "Apology accepted." He felt kind of dorky saying it, but felt he needed to acknowledge the apology.

It was early, but since everyone was there, Abe decided to call the meeting scheduled for after dinner to order now.

Leonard learned that Cille had been volunteering at the animal shelter and met the others through contacts there with other volunteer agencies. Tom and Liv had been living in a homeless shelter. Cille needed a place for her collection of stray cats and her house was too small and more than she could take care of after her husband died. Abe was in the Theater Guild and volunteered at a soup kitchen associated with the homeless shelter. He had contacts in the local government and Cille had known a Realtor and those contacts led to an eccentric landowner who owned the mill. The owner had been looking for someone to act more as security to keep it from being vandalized or to keep anyone getting hurt on the property. Cille and Abe talked to the mill owner and convinced him they and other designees would act as live-in caretakers and would actually lease the place for a dollar a year and that dollar also gave them the right of first refusal if the owner ever decided to sell the property. The only potential problem was that the owner was old and no one was quite sure who would get the property when he died. He had set up a trust to pay the taxes, so at least that wasn't a concern.

So, Cille and Abe had moved in about a year and a half ago. Shortly after that Boris and Natsha came and just about a year ago Morrie, Richard and Jill showed up and Jill seemed totally smitten by Richard and they moved in together after a month or so. That was a controversial move within the group too, because Cille and Abe were fundamentalist Christians who thought homosexuality was a sin. Eventually they agreed to hate the sin and love the sinner. Abe had pointed out that God hated divorce too, and according to the Bible, anyone who divorced and remarried while the ex- was still alive was committing adultery and living in sin. That pretty much killed the objections and Richard and Jill were finally allowed to stay after their "guest" status had ended. Tom and Liv moved in just after Richard and Jill had, while Richard and Jill were still "guests".

Guest status was apparently where a tenant started out and then at some time, not a set period or after any certain conditions were met, just at mutual agreement, the guest met with the rest of the group and they voted to accept or reject the guest as a permanent resident.. No one really could tell Leonard what happened if a guest was rejected, as it had not come up before, but the consensus seemed to be that they would not be asked to actually leave, but would continue on as a guest until they left of their own accord, or were voted in. Members had to have unanimous approval. Leonard doubted that any of this would hold up in a court of law, but the whole thing was pretty quasi-legal or "extra" legal anyhow.

To date there had been very little structure, but important things seemed to get done. About the only thing so far where they came together as a team was the evening meal, but the preparation was done mostly by the women and Jill and the gardening was also mostly done by the women, although Abe did a lot in the garden and Jill tended part of an herb garden that Cille and Natasha had started. Jill also had a couple fruit trees and some grapes that were outside of the mill proper.

Boris and Richard had built the solar heated shower and the primitive privies. Abe and Richard had built some partitions with Jill's help. Boris was working on plans for several things, but nothing concrete had been done—the elevator, a power system, plumbing, heat. There was a huge coal fired boiler for the building, but they hadn't used it because it was so big and no one knew quite how to run it. They had made it through last winter by all living on third floor and using kerosene space heaters.

Money was pooled, but very loosely—there seemed to be no rules that anyone had to give any set amount or all they had or whatever. Everyone but Tom and Liv seemed to have pensions or some sort of bank accounts with money that they shared pretty freely. Leonard had half of the insurance money from the fire and some investments. He had been self employed, so he got half of the investments he and his wife had made while they were married, plus what he had put in when he left a government planning job to get married and then became self employed, working several years as a framing carpenter, a home remodeler, a substitute teacher, a jeweler, an artist and writer (darn little income doing those two though!). Before the government planning job in transportation planning, he had worked for the government in housing, community development, solid waste planning, community corrections planning, did a stint as a manager and route planner for a transit authority, worked at an oil refinery, a landscape nursery, drew house plans, and worked in an iron fabricating plant.

He found out that the person who came closest to having as an eclectic job history as he had was Abe, who had been an actor, a trumpet player in a nightclub, and apparently a teacher of some sort. He had also worked on a farm "in his younger days" and in a library, where he lied and said he was AMLS accredited.

Boris had been an engineer in one of the Slovakian countries and so had Natasha. Richard taught at a high school in a neighboring community (Leonard thought every girl in his class must have had a crush on him—he had the looks of a young Richard Widmark—and that led Leonard to wonder if he was no longer teaching because of some impropriety with a student) and Jill was an interior designer. Morrie was a retired accountant. He fit the stereotype of an accountant, mousy and frumpish.

It was unclear what work experience Tom or Liv had had. Tom said something about working on "the line" somewhere and it seemed like Liv had done similar work—perhaps in the same factory. Their lives were sort of vague. But Leonard figured his life was sort of vague too—or improbable. Most people did not believe he could have had so many jobs. When they learned he was older than he looked, that helped, but still, holding so many jobs in less than forty years stretched his credibility. At an interview for a position at a regional commission in Grand Rapids, the director had looked at his resume and asked if there were a job he hadn't had and he thought quickly and said, "Yes--lion tamer." He told people later that he had realized that wasn't even quite true, as he had worked as a substitute teacher.

Someone once told him that they hadn't believed he had had so many jobs, figured he had just read a lot about them, but he knew so many details when he talked about them, they figured it was just as hard to believe that he had such a good memory for what he'd read. He gave him his standard line, "Well, I do have a photographic memory, but it's not fully developed." One man he was talking to about his work in Port City said, "You worked for Port County?—I knew the Treasurer there and he was exactly as you described him!" (Leonard had told the man that the description of an 'ignorant and proud of it,' foul mouthed, racist, sexist pig would have fit most of the people in positions of power in Port City, so that was no big accomplishment to accurately describe the Treasurer! The man agreed with him.)

Leonard suggested to the group at the mill that they organize their time, assign priorities to projects and assign teams to projects by priority. He suggested too that people be given long weekends off from projects to start with so they didn't burn out. Someone suggested having another meeting to do these things and he objected, saying that was what people do when they want to pretend they are doing something. "Really, it's easier to define things right away and set your priorities. When I was a planner, the thing we all dreaded was monthly status reports. I found that if I did what we called a boiler plate report—a template or outline, all I had to do was fill in the blanks as I went through the month. The report was pretty much written by the end of the month and I could work on more important things. Defining a task really does help—prevents useless effort on things that aren't pertinent to the task. Anyway, enough talk…."

As he used to say when writing minutes, "discussion followed."

It being Friday, they agreed to take the weekend to rest and think and meet again on Sunday evening to schedule work and then again on Monday to follow up to see how things were progressing.

They finished the meeting around 10 and after strolling out to pee and to get a container to use as a chamber pot, Leonard went up to his "room". He took off his clothes and put on a t-shirt and drawstring pants to sleep in. Bundling up the clothes he'd taken off, he thought about laundry. He'd have to talk to them about that.

In the morning Leonard woke up and after attending to nature's call, he decided to explore the grounds.

His usual depression that plagued him when he wasn't busy descended upon him and he found himself once again fighting suicidal thoughts. He went into the lunchroom and made coffee. He grew bored just sitting and decided to go back out to the courtyard to explore. The morning was warm and sunny and he decided to do tai chi while he had the quiet time to himself. When he was through and his mind was a little clearer, he was thinking about one of the main precepts of tai chi—that there is a path and it opens to those who are ready. He thought he saw a path through the overgrown weeds and began following it. He expected it to lead to one of the other accessory buildings or to the coal fired plant along the railroad siding, but it led between them and he thought it must not really lead anywhere, because it curved back towards the side of the main building.

Then he saw that it went down a steep rocky path and that the building itself sat on a deeper foundation than he had thought—it appeared that there was much more than a one-story basement under it. Where the ground on this side fell away towards the rushing river below, he saw and old stone foundation. Then he saw the waterwheel. Once he saw that, he wondered where the supply of water had come from, because now it was high and dry and only a weedy ravine lead from it down to the river. He scrambled down the stony slope, wondering if maybe he should go back and at least write a note so they'd know where to find his body if he slipped and fell, but he'd come this far and he didn't want to go back.

Then he saw the first pier; a stone foundation with a broken off wood structure coming out of it. He looked further up the slope and thought he glimpsed another several yards away. He scrambled up the slope and found it. Climbing up onto that one, he was able to see a series of them leading up the ravine, some of them still had much of their wooden superstructure, including what he was looking for—a flume. When he had seen this from the roof, he had thought it was a railroad trestle, but now its purpose was clear—it was a flume to bring water from upstream down to the waterwheel. He looked back at the mill. Yes, that had to be it. The mill wheel was protected by a roof and just looked like a shed on the side of the mill. He wanted to explore further, but the rumbling in his stomach made him decide to go back and see about something for breakfast and to perhaps enlist the help of some able-bodied explorers—and to find out if anyone knew where the flume began—where were the headwaters of this millrace? Seemed like it couldn't be very far.

He was enthused with the idea of rebuilding the flume, but then thought of the near impossibility of rebuilding a structure made from timbers the size of telephone poles. A flume was one thing, but building something on the order of the Bridge on the River Kwi seemed pretty daunting. He wondered how far the flume ran, but his view ahead was blocked by trees and a steep incline. He looked back and saw that at the crow flies, he had only gone a hundred yards or so. He started back the same way he had come, but was wondering if there were a roadway or even a path back to the mill on the high ground.

He looked and saw something like a deer runway along the side of the ravine. It branched off a few yards back from where he was, so he went back and followed it. It was a difficult climb; the path was narrow and he was no deer. But he had followed similar trails while hunting along a river in Michigan on some land his dad owned. His father's land had had a river and some steep log roll-offs left from the lumbering era.

He stopped occasionally to look back and each time was surprised at how far he had advanced upward. He judged by the sun that it must be about 10:00 and people might be up an around. He looked ahead and saw another wooden support on the steep hill ahead. Maybe the headwater for the flume was at the top of the hill. That thought pushed him to go up the last thirty feet or so to the ridge above him. When he reached it, he was on the shoulder of a road.

Ahead was a sign that said, "Mill Pond Park, City of Grover's Corners, est. 1958." He walked to the park entrance and saw a surprisingly large pond. He walked along the road a short distance into the park to a sign with an arrow. When he got closer he read "Grover Falls." He was too tired to explore further and still wanted to walk back to the mill, so he turned around and followed the road back out of the park and eastward back toward the mill (he hoped). After a short hike, the road turned to the right, but he recognized the place from when he came in yesterday and followed an unmarked gravel road that angled to the left and down towards the mill. Within a short distance he could see the mill. He was tired, thirsty and sweaty by the time he got back and went into the lunch room. Natasha was fixing a cup of tea and asked if he would like some. "Maybe later—I need just cool water right now—I just hiked down by the river and up to the mill pond." He got the mug he had used last night and filled it from the water jug and drank it down.

"You must be very thirsty!" said Natasha. "That is far from here, no?"

"Not far as the crow flies, but lots of steep parts to climb." He filled the cup and emptied it again. "What kind of tea is that? Looks like 'Red Zinger'."

"It is very similar—it has hibiscus flowers that give it the red color, like 'Red Zinger' and it has lemon grass, but also has some other herbs."

"May I try it?" He held out his cup and she poured it full. He sipped it. Not bad. "I like something called 'Monk's Blend' that is similar to this."

"This is, in fact, my version of 'Monk's Blend'. It is made mostly from the herbs we grow here, but I did get some of the less common ones from a shop in the village."

"Very nice. Thank you." He looked around hopefully, "Umm, I don't suppose there are donuts or bagels or anything like that around...?

She wrinkled her nose and replied, "Those all have a high glycemic index, bad for your health."

"Yeah, I suppose so. I guess I'll go into town and see what I can find, but first I should take a shower. Will anyone mind, do you suppose?"

"No one will be showering in the morning—too cold."

"Then I guess I won't have to fight anyone to get to it!" He put his mug back and thanked her for the tea.

She was right, the water was breathtakingly cold, but he felt refreshed when he had washed off the sweat. He walked from the plastic tarped enclosure to grab his towel and was surprised to see Natasha watching him. He paused for a moment with the towel in front of him.

"Go ahead and dry yourself. I just wanted to see you without clothes." Natasha said in an off hand, matter of fact way.

He began toweling off, pretending she was a doctor or something. "If I said the same thing to you, would you let me see you naked?"

"Sure," she replied. "Would you like to see me naked?"

"Is the Pope Catholic?" Then thinking she might not know this expression, he added, "Hell yes, what man wouldn't?"

She laughed and began taking her clothes off as she walked towards him. He was seeing her less "doctoral" now and was conscious of his biological response. She smiled and came up to him, her body still in bra and panties against his and touched his penis. "My husband apparently doesn't like so much to see me naked." She stroked Leonard, "You, on the other hand," she squeezed him to let him know which hand she meant, "seem to like it."

"Well, yeah," Leonard croaked, "But…."

"Yes, speaking of butt…" She tuned away and slipped her panties down and bent over slowly to remove them from around her feet. Still bent down, she turned slightly to look around her legs at Leonard. "You like this butt?"

Leonard wanted to jump her right then and there and managed to whisper, "Is that a trick question?" before he did.

He felt guilty about it immediately after the sex. The rationalizations that he was only human, had been without female companionship for months, and all the rest didn't help. As they dressed he told he how he felt and that he was sorry he had taken advantage of her. She laughed, "I believe that it was I who seduced you! No need for remorse—and my husband wouldn't care even if he did find out, and I won't be telling him, will you?"

"Absolutely not, but…"

"Ah, those buts get you into trouble each time!" She wiggled hers as she walked away.

Leonard had only thought he was hungry before, the cold shower (so much for that theory, he thought) and the sexual activity on top of the morning walk had made him ravenous and some tofu and a couple lettuce leaves weren't going to help much. He went back down to the courtyard and was getting into his car when Jill slammed out of the building and down the step into the courtyard. He seemed upset and walked right up to Leonard. When Jill got closer, Leonard could see his nose was red and his face tear streaked. "Are you okay, Jill?"

Jill sighed, "I'm fine, just a little spat with Richard. You wouldn't be going into town by any chance, would you?"

"Yes, I thought I would get some breakfast somewhere— hop in if you'd like, maybe you can direct me to a good place to eat?"

Jill got in and Leonard turned the car around and as he approached the gate Liv ran out towards the car and waved at him. He stopped and she came over to his side and leaned in the open window. She was wearing a loose fitting top and no bra and Leonard got a good look at her pert breasts. He pulled his eyes up to look her in the eye and she seemed to be unaware of his struggle. "Hey, can I bum a ride too?"

"Climb in," he said and she got into the back seat and pulled a pack of cigarettes and a lighter out of her bag.

He looked at her in the mirror and said, "I'd appreciate it if you could hold off on smoking until you're out of the car. If you don't mind."

She sighed loudly, and settled moodily into the rear seat, but put the cigarettes away. Jill turned to Leonard and mouthed, "Thanks."

He didn't know if Jill's thanks were for the ride or for his asking Liv not to smoke. When they got to the gate, both passengers sat unmoving, so Leonard jumped out and opened it, then jumped back in and drove through. He started to get out again to close it. Jill said it would be okay if he wouldn't be gone long. So he drove on.

He passed a little restaurant and asked Jill if it were any good, "Oh, darlin' don't even ask; that place is pretty 'red,' keep going; there's a little place I know of just inside the town off the main drag." She emphasized "drag" and Leonard realized she had done it unconsciously.

Leonard looked for some sort of confirmation from Liv, but she was chewing on her nails. She suddenly arched her back and pressing against the seat, lifted her bottom up and spread her legs. Leonard quickly looked back to the road, but noticed her pulling the skintight jeans out of her butt crack. He licked his lips and saw that somehow none of this had escaped Jill. She patted his hand. He felt like he was in a scene from the movie "Beguiled" where the wounded Union soldier stumbles into a school or something where several women had taken refuge and becomes the object of all their affection. He hoped his experience ended better than Eastwood's had—in the movie a little girl poisoned him with mushrooms after he accidentally killed her pet turtle.

He wanted to talk, but didn't want to talk about Jill's spat in front of Liv, and Liv seemed distracted, alternately biting her lip, chewing her nails or picking at her scalp.

Soon they were in the "business district" of the town and Jill said, "See the tanning salon up on the left at the light? Turn there." So he did.

"Okay, you can park anywhere here—see that restaurant? 'Tony's'? That's got good food and good service...."

Liv snorted and Leonard looked at her in the mirror, but she was not meeting his gaze. "What about you, where are you headed?" he asked no one in particular.

"I'll just get out here. If you're here when I get back, could I have a ride back to the mill?" Jill said, smiling. *God, he was beautiful.* Leonard couldn't see how he could feel that way after having just had sex with a woman who was pretty spectacular, and knowing this person was not a woman. *Beautiful nonetheless.*

Liv was already out and mumbled thanks. He called after her—"If you need a ride back, I'll probably be here about 45 minutes..." Having lit a cigarette already, she waved it distractedly as she walked away.

Leonard got out of the car and Jill was already gone. He walked into the restaurant, not knowing just what to expect. It was dark and cool, clean and quiet and fairly well filled. A waitress called to him to sit anywhere.

It became obvious that the place was a place where gay men gathered. Leonard got some looks as he entered, but figured a lot of that would happen in any small town establishment when a stranger walked in. He sat in the far corner so he could see the place and was away from the glare coming in the window. Bright light gave him migraines. A waiter came over with a glass of ice water and a menu. He asked him to bring him a regular coffee. He said, "We just brewed a pot of hazelnut, if you'd like to try that?"

"Sure," he said, remembering how his dad and he would drink a pot of hazelnut coffee between them when they had breakfast together. They had done that almost every Thursday morning for years, after Leonard had moved to the same city where he had grown up after he married Peggy. He had known Peggy in high school and when he got reacquainted with her at a high school reunion and found out she was divorced, one thing led to another, they got married and ultimately they divorced.

The menu had the standard fare, but with a bit of flair, items such as omelets with fresh vegetables inside, French toast with cream cheese and preserves folded in, and bagels with cream cheese and lox, freshly squeezed juice, etc. He drank his coffee and thought about what to eat, while observing the place. Nothing noteworthy was going on and when the waitress returned he ordered an omelet with cheddar cheese and ham, redskin potatoes with herb butter and their version of V-8 made with freshly juiced vegetables.

The waiter asked him if he were new in town, as he hadn't seen him in before and he had an accent. Leonard told him that he was staying at the mill at the edge of town and that Jill who lived there had told him about this place. "Jill said you have excellent food." This was a bit of an exaggeration, but the waiter seemed pleased.

Leonard was surprised when the waiter sat down in the booth across from him and leaned in conspiratorially, "So, you know Jill do you?" He toyed with his earring. "How well do you know her?"

"Not well at all," Leonard was always leery of people who seemed to be pumping him for information and remembered the time he went to the bar with his boss and a new hire, Cal, who was rumored to be a "trouble shooter" who rooted out disloyal employees. Ed and Cal had plied Leonard with booze and asked him about other employees. To every name that was brought up, Leonard had said they were excellent employees. Meanwhile, Ed and Cal were getting noticeably inebriated.

Ed began telling a story about when he was in a bar in Tangiers and there was a naked woman on stage and they were burning her with cigars. Cal said very loudly, "I would have stuck it up her ass!" Everyone in the bar turned to look at them and Ed literally covered his face and looked down and Leonard learned more than he cared to about either one of them.

The waiter interrupted Leonard's thoughts and said, "Is she still seeing that Richard person?"

Leonard had many thoughts go through his head—what did he mean by "seeing"? He figured he knew why the waitress called Jill "she," but he also thought about Jill that morning, fleeing to his car in a state of turmoil. In the last split second the thought that none of this was any of the waiter's business and he said, "I really don't know. Guess you should ask Jill when you see her."

The waiter gave Leonard a withering look and stood up. If he was going to say anything else, he stopped and followed Leonard's gaze to see that Jill had just walked through the door and was letting his eyes adjust to the dimness. Leonard gave a small wave and Jill smiled and flounced over to the table as the waiter melted away.

"Hello, sweet cakes, mind if I join you?" Seeing Leonard smile and indicate the seat, Jill threw himself into the booth. "Have you ordered yet?"

"No, not yet. Just getting to know the wait staff."

"Oh, Raul." He pronounced it "Ra-ool" and with a dismissive tone.

"What do you recommend?" asked Leonard.

"Definitely *not* Raul." Jill said with a sigh as she took off her sunglasses, pausing to look at Leonard over the tops of them as he did so.

Leonard laughed and said, "Well, I'm hungry, but not that hungry." He found himself embarrassed to have said it.

Jill replied, "Darling, let's hope you never get *that* hungry!"

Leonard was so tempted to fall into Jill's way of speaking, to reply, "Oh, you silly!" but managed to restrain himself. Instead he said, "He's not my type."

Jill looked at him again, as if analyzing just what he meant. Raul showed up again and stood on one foot, hand on hip and flipped open an order pad. "Have we decided what we're having?"

"I'd like a hot set of cinnamon buns, but I see you don't have them," Jill said innocently, "So I guess I'll have the French toast with strawberries. And, I'd like to just devour a juicy Polska kielbasa, but I'll settle for sausage links." He licked his lips, alluringly.

Leonard innocently cleared his throat and Raul who looked like he was going to say something to Jill, decided not to and turned to Leonard. "May I recommend our tart? On second thought, it's not that good," Raul said, turning slightly towards Jill.

"Oh, darling, you'll never kn…."

Leonard quickly interrupted, "I'd like a ham and cheddar cheese omelet, redskin potatoes and a glass of your vegetable juice." He hoped this wasn't being translated into something he didn't intend. "Oh, and more coffee, please." He gave Raul what he hoped would be seen as an understanding smile.

Raul turned on his heel and Leonard drank another sip of his coffee. He looked across his cup at Jill and said, "You are *bad*."

Jill smiled coyly, "When I'm good, I'm very good; but when I'm bad, I'm better."

"I guess I'll never know."

"You'll never know unless you try."

"I don't swing that way, but if I did…"

"Listen to you!" Jill lowered his voice and added a gruffness to it that Leonard found was both unfair and sounded more like Shirley Temple than it sounded like him, 'I don't swing that way!'" Then in his normal voice, if indeed he was ever normal, Jill added, "Sounds like dialog from a Raymond Chandler novel or something. Or maybe from 'The Boys in the Band.'"

"I like Raymond Chandler, and I did see 'Boys in the Band' way back in college."

"Well, aren't you egalitarian!"

Leonard sighed, "Look, I'm not trying to pick a fight with you. If I've said anything…"

"Oh, don't…" Jill said, "I'm just feeling catty. Richard is such a tool sometimes."

"Ah, I couldn't help but notice that you two seemed to have had a spat. Now's your chance to make him jealous—Raul is eager…"

"Oh, puleeze!"

"Sorry." Leonard added, "It's really unfair of me to talk about Raul either. He seems like a perfectly nice chap, but not your type."

"You said he wasn't your type either, so doesn't that make you, ipso facto, my type?" countered Jill.

"Umm, I think your logic is flawed…" But Leonard reached across the table and patted Jill's hand. *"What am I doing?"* he thought and pulled his hand back. "If ever I was tempted, it…" He stopped when he saw that Raul had returned with the food, with the usual waiterly knack for showing up when you least wanted them. Leonard picked up his coffee cup to show Raul it was empty, but Raul was already walking away, hips swinging, oblivious.

Leonard continued, "Even if…it wouldn't be fair for so many reasons. The main thing is that I am just attracted to you because you are pretty in a feminine way…I mean…."

"Don't analyze it, Leonard. And thanks." Then he viciously speared a sausage with his fork, causing Leonard to almost wince in sympathy, but then brought it to his lips and inserted it provocatively. "Besides, I am monogamous, though someone I could name doesn't seem to be."

Leonard thought he meant Richard, but wasn't exactly sure.

Jill added, "But if you ever wanted to try something a little different, in words you might understand, 'take a walk on the wild side,' I'd be able to fit you in." He popped the sausage into his mouth and Leonard pried his eyes off Jill and looked back at his own plate and hurriedly took a forkful. He needed more coffee, since they didn't serve alcohol.

Jill said, "Honey, we need more coffee here!"

Leonard looked up to see Raul trudge by and he sighed and filled Leonard's cup. Leonard thanked him, giving him a big smile. In his mind, Leonard had been showering him with blue light since he sensed that Raul was unhappy and was beginning to lose hope when Raul smiled back.

Leonard felt that he had gotten to know a couple people at the mill, but still felt that several were still ciphers. He was going to ask Jill about Tom and Liv, but just then, Liv walked in, and like everyone else, stood for a time to let her eyes adjust. Leonard told Jill that Liv had just come in and waved to her.

Jill said to Leonard, "And we were having such a nice conversation!"

Liv walked over and plunked herself down next to Leonard.

Jill said, "Well, I have a couple errands to run, but I would like a ride back. Can I meet you at your car in about a half hour?"

"Sure," said Leonard. Jill snatched her check from the table and left after stopping to pay at the cash register in front. She gave Leonard a little wave as she walked through the door. Leonard still saw Jill as "her" and not "him." He had wanted to ask Jill about that, but didn't quite know how to broach the subject. What does one say? "Hey, air you a boy or air you a girl?" Or, "Say, you are a right pretty thing!" Or, "I'd like to paint your mouth…" he blinked those thoughts away and turned to Liv.

"What's new with you?" he asked.

She stood up and he thought he had said something to make her leave, but she sat down where Jill had been sitting and noticing Leonard's reaction said, "I just like to sit so I can see the person I'm talking too."

"Yeah, so do I…" said Leonard, conversationally. He was afraid to say anything that might set her off. "Would you like a menu; coffee…?"

She shook her head, then said, "Well, I would like some tea and maybe a muffin, but I'm a little low on cash…."

"Not a problem, my treat."

He waved to Raul, who gave him another long-suffering look and ambled over.

"Could you bring a cup of tea and a muffin over for the lady?" Leonard asked him.

"I could. Would you like me to?"

Leonard smiled tautly, "Yes, if it isn't too much trouble."

"What kind of tea would the lady like?"

"Oh, I don't know…."

Raul stalked off and returned with a menu, "When you've figured out what you want, just give me a whistle."

Leonard half expected the rest of the Bacall line from "Casa Blanca," but was relieved when Raul just walked demurely away.

Liv looked over the menu and said, "I'm hungrier than I thought, now that I've seen the menu…do you mind if I get something besides a muffin?"

"Not at all."

She waved to Raul and he returned, order pad in hand and stood on one foot, hip jutted impatiently. Liv ordered steak and eggs, hash browns, white toast and a muffin and apricot nectar tea.

"So, how do you like living at the mill?" Leonard asked her after Raul had left.

"It's okay."

"How long have you been there?"

"Oh…about a year I guess." She thought for a moment, playing with her hair. "Yeah, Tom and I moved in just before winter last year."

Leonard didn't know what else to say without appearing to be prying, so he asked her if she were from around there originally. She said she had lived in Grover's Corners all her life.

Raul brought a little silver teapot of hot water, and a cup with a packaged tea bag in it. Liv took the teabag out of the wrapper and poured the hot water on it. She poked at it with her spoon.

"The people are kind of odd though…" she said.

"The people in Grover's Corners, or the people at the mill?" Leonard asked.

"Well, both, really, but I was thinking of the people at the mill. You know, Abe, with that top hat and all…"

"Yeah, he's a character, all right! But good hearted! Seems like a very caring kind of guy."

"I guess." She sipped her tea. "And that Natasha—like some gypsy queen or something. Can hardly understand her sometimes with that put-on accent."

"Oh, I thought that was real…" Leonard said in such a way that he hoped she would take the hint that Natasha's accent was not made-up, adding, "She seems to know Russian."

"Well, I wouldn't know. She sounds like a cartoon character to me."

"It just dawned on me that you probably aren't old enough to remember Boris and Natasha from 'The Rocky and Bullwinkle' cartoon show. That's why they call her Natasha, because they already had Boris, so it would be natural for her to be Natasha."

"So her name isn't Natasha?" said Liv.

"Oh, I thought everyone knew that—no, her real name is Irena or something—shoot, I know it isn't 'Irena', but I've already forgotten. Anyway, people just started calling her

Natasha after the cartoon character and it stuck…I wonder how long they've been there?"

"You writin' a book or something?" Liv said, but Leonard couldn't tell if she meant to be sarcastic.

"No, just curious. Speaking of names, Richard's is unusual…"

"What do you mean?" Liv asked.

"Oh, uh, 'Richard Corey' is a name from a poem—a poem about a rich socialite that everyone envies because he's got it all. The rich guy in the poem is named 'Richard Corey'."

"Oh. I wouldn't know; I was never big into poetry. And rich socialite hardly fits Richard."

Leonard decided not to pursue the strangeness of Liv's name. "How's the tea?"

"It's surprisingly good, really. But the water isn't hot enough."

"It never is. Those little teapots just don't seem to hold the heat."

"Yeah, I've noticed that…"

Raul interrupted by slapping the plate of food down between them. "And I suppose you want more coffee."

"If it wouldn't be too much trouble." Leonard waited till Raul left and as he stood up, said to Liv, "I have to use the rest room—recycle some of this coffee."

"I hear ya."

"Oh, Natasha's real name is Theomina…" he said and walked toward the restrooms.

When he came back he was surprised to see that Liv had finished her plate of food and was wrapping the muffin in a napkin. She put it in her purse. The ever solicitous Raul followed Leonard and put another pot of hot water down on the table with another tea bag. Liv unwrapped and dunked the teabag in the water. Raul told her the second teabag was extra and Leonard said, "Just add it to the bill and give it to me."

Liv excused herself to use the lady's room. Leonard looked at the clock above the cash register. He guessed a half hour hadn't passed and figured that Jill could wait a bit anyway.

Liv returned and dawdled over her tea. Leonard asked her if she knew anything about the mill pond up in the park on the hill.

"Just that it's a great place to park and make out."

"You don't know whether the city ever used the falls to generate electricity, do you?"

"No, wouldn't know anything about that."

He figured next time he was in town he'd ask at the city hall and see if anyone there might know. He made a point of looking at the clock and said, "Well, I should be getting back. You are welcome to come along."

He paid the bill and went to the car. Jill was standing next to it and got in when he saw them approach. Leonard wondered if anyone else had a car. While it seemed anachronistic that Abe would drive one, it also seemed anachronistic to see him on a Segway.

When they returned to the mill, Leonard found Abe and Cille sitting in lawn chairs up on the top roof, enjoying the sun and sipping on drinks. They invited him to join them and poured him a tall drink from their pitcher. They all agreed that it was a lovely day.

Leonard sat and chatted idly with them for a few moments, then said "Another thing I was wondering about, and hope you don't mind discussing 'business' on your day off…"

"I don't really separate business from pleasure—it's all part of living. Please continue," said Abe.

"Well, first, did you know that there is a waterwheel on the lowest level of this building?"

Abe nodded and Cille said, "There is?"

Abe turned to Cill—"Yes, dear, it is there, but you have to walk around the building to see it, and even then you see the housing for it and may think it's just a shed added onto the building. I didn't see it until I walked down by the creek one day to see if I could do some fishing."

"Well, not only is there a waterwheel, but there are the ruins of the flume that runs to it," Leonard continued.

"Yes, nicely built. Must have been quite a feat of engineering in their day" said Abe.

"Yes. Initially I had thought we could repair it, but it would be a daunting task, though I think it *could* be done. But, when I followed the ruins of the flume to the containment pond, I saw that the village owned the pond and there is a falls."

"Yes, that's right," Abe said.

"Well, I was thinking that instead of rebuilding the flume and running the waterwheel for just us, and getting riparian rights and all that that would go along with it, maybe we could do something with the village to construct a water turbine at the base of the falls and produce electricity in a cooperative venture so everyone could benefit, not just us. Seems like rebuilding the flume and getting the waterwheel running again just to supply the mill here with power is a lot of work for little benefit. But, getting a turbine up and running to provide electricity for the whole community would be really good!"

"I like how you think! Wouldn't that be grand? Have hydroelectric power for the whole village. And, it would be non-polluting!"

"The thing is, they may be reluctant to do anything—what is the source of power to generate their electricity right now?" asked Leonard.

"Well, I think they get it from the grid on a contractual basis, if I remember correctly, but they village council had been talking about a coal fired plant..."

Abe offered Leonard another drink and as he lifted the pitcher, said, "Maybe you and Boris could present a proposal to the council..."

Suddenly Boris appeared as if summoned like a demon by the mention of his name. Red-faced, he ran up to Leonard and grabbed him and pulled him out of his chair, screaming, "Don't ever touch my wife again or I will kill you!" Leonard pushed Boris off and brushed spittle from his face. They glared at one another for a moment while Abe and Cille looked from Leonard to Boris and back in amazement, and then Boris stalked off.

After Boris left, Leonard sat down shakily in the chair again. "I'll take the refill you offered..." and held out his glass.

Abe poured him another screwdriver. "If you need to talk about what just happened, it may help you sort things out..."

"I would like that—after I've gotten my heart rate back under 200 perhaps...." He added, nervously, "I hope this incident doesn't jeopardize my staying here..."

Partially to change the subject, Leonard asked them about the transportation situation. Cille told him that at the moment Richard had a sports car and she and Abe had a van and both were kept in one of the outbuildings. Leonard told them that he had been thinking of offering his car for general use, with the proviso that anyone who used it just fill it with gas before returning it and just keeping the keys on a hook in the lunch room.

"What a generous offer!" said Abe. "That would be wonderful, as the van is big and doesn't get good gas mileage to just run into town with to buy a paper or whatnot. And hardly anyone would know how to drive Richard's sport's car, plus it is too small to get more than two people in, and," he held his hand up to his mouth to talk as an aside, "I don't think Richard would be that keen on the hoi polloi using his baby...."

Richard burst through the door and sprinted up to Leonard. Leonard was on his feet before Richard got to him. Richard stopped short and said, "You just stay away from Jill...or...just stay away!" He turned on his heel and stormed back the way he came.

Abe looked at Leonard, "My, haven't you have been a busy lad this morning!"

Leonard dropped back into the chair and Abe poured him another drink, emptying the pitcher. "Cille, do you mind?" He handed her the pitcher and she gave Leonard a knowing smile and wiggled her fanny provocatively as she sashayed away.

Leonard tore his eyes away and looked at Abe, who was once again studying him. "You know, one of my favorite philosophers once said, 'You can observe a lot just by looking,'..."

"I'm innocent—well, in the second case anyway... and Cille and I are just friends...and didn't Yogi Bera say that?"

Abe looked at Leonard over his bi-focals, "Did I say otherwise?"

Leonard looked around expectantly—"Well, where is he?"

"Where's who?" Abe asked.

"Yogi Berra—everyone else you've mentioned so far has popped out of the woodwork to spit beer in my ear, so…"

Abe gave a hearty laugh. Then laughed even harder as Cille returned with the refilled pitcher in one hand and a fresh bottle of vodka in the other, wearing a baseball cap. "What?" she asked. Then seeing them pointing at her NY Yankees ball cap said, "The sun is bright!"

Abe held out his glass for a refill. He looked at Leonard questioningly and Leonard said, "I think I've had enough!"

"Well, you certainly have added interest to our normal, 'run of the mill' morning!" said Abe. "It is good to have you around. Just maybe try to keep it in your pants for a while, anyway!"

Cille nudged Abe, but touched Leonard under the table with her foot. She winked at Leonard and he gulped the rest of his drink.

Leonard stood up. "Thank you for not saying Tom's name out loud!" he said to Abe.

Abe laughed and indicated that Leonard should look behind him as Cille said, "My, my…!" in a tone of wonderment.

Leonard turned and said, "I didn't do it!"

"Do what?" said Tom.

"Oh, nothing…" replied Leonard.

Tom went over to the garden area and came back suddenly and Leonard could see he was angry and said under his breath, "Oh shit, what did I do now?"

"Ah," said Abe, looking at Tom and in a voice loud enough for him to hear, "You've probably noticed that your pot plants are gone."

Leonard turned from Tom to Abe and Tom turned from looking at Leonard to looking at Abe. "Yes, I cannot tell a lie…" Abe turned to Cille and in an aside said, "Would that be considered a mixed metaphor?" and turning back to Tom said, "I chopped down your hemp plants. You know the rules. I don't have any problem with people using recreational drugs, but the government does and we are abiding by their rules in this place. You agreed to that when you came here. Enough people in the town don't like us here and want us gone—that would only offer them a legal reason to get rid of us."

"How would they even have known? Way up on this roof?"

"I don't know if they would. Maybe someone would tell them, maybe they have spy satellites, how would I know? But that isn't the issue, the issue is that you agreed. And now there is no issue. 'Here lies Les Moore, four shots with a forty-four; no Les, no Moore.'"

Tom turned on his heel and marched away.

"Well, welcome to my world," said Leonard to Abe as they watched Tom pound through the stairway door and heard his footsteps retreating on the stairs.

"Just one big happy family. 'A nation divided cannot stand,'" said Abe.

"Was that Yogi Berra, or Thomas Jefferson?"

"That was me," said Abe, ambiguously.

"Well," said Leonard, "I am tired from all of this and am going to my place to take a nap."

Abe held up his hand for him to wait and poured a powder into Leonard's empty glass and then filled it with water. "Prevents hangover…trust me."

Leonard had no reason not to trust him, so he gulped the concoction down and thanked Abe and Cille for the drinks. Leonard stumbled down the stairs to fifth floor and fell into his bed for a nap. He fell asleep wondering if he should be worried about the threats, his mind apparently having decided everything was okay. His last conscious though was that he was too inebriated to talk sense and the people were too angry to listen. He'd try later.

He woke up and couldn't remember where he was for a moment. He wondered how long he had slept as he put his feet on the floor and sat on the edge of his bed. He could see through the abundant windows that it was still light out. He had felt much better before he took his nap than he did now, but he wasn't as bad off as he expected when he remembered how many screwdrivers he'd downed in such a short time. He'd have to find out what that was that Abe had given him. He was thirsty and had to pee. He stood up, a little unsteady on his feet and then he saw the shape of someone by the doorway to the stairs. His heart raced, wondering if it was one of the guys who had threatened him.

"Leonardo, it is me…" The voice was unmistakable—it was Natasha.

"Natasha, I don't think it is a good idea for you to be here— Boris is very angry with me!"

"I knocked on the door, but I don't know if you heard me. We must talk."

"Okay, but not here. Let me meet you in a more public place—Boris is plenty mad enough already without our adding to it!"

"I know, and I am sorry…," Natasha said. "Yes, you are right. I will go downstairs and we can talk in the lunchroom."

"Good, I'll be down shortly."

After the door closed, Leonard went to the floor drain and relieved his aching bladder and then walked to the stairs.

He went downstairs to the lunch room and Natasha was sitting with a cup of tea. She stood up, "Why don't we go outside to talk?"

When they got to the courtyard she turned to him. "I don't know what happened—why Boris got so angry with you. I heard from Cille that he did. Leonardo, I know for a fact that he does not care for me. I know this for several reasons." They had been walking side by side and she stopped and turned toward Leonard and looked him in the eye. "First, I know because he married me only to get into the country. I was citizen and he wanted to live in United States. My Uncle knows him back in Russia, and so we were introduced and the arrangement was made. Secondly, Boris is a homosexual. He has not touched me since we have been married. Touched me, you know...." She trailed off while Leonard nodded. They were by his car and he leaned against it

"One more thing..." she continued, her eyebrows furrowed with concern, "Boris is bad man. And he is strong—how you say, tough guy—a fighter. I have reason to believe he is involved in secret politzia. I cannot say more about zis." Her accent got thicker as she talked about things related to her past. She grasped Leonard's arm, in a surprisingly strong grip, "I don't know if his anger was real or for show, but be careful of him. And, if you need someone to confide in, I would trust Abe and maybe Cille, but no one else. I believe Boris and Jill may be lovers."

Leonard raised his eyebrows. Obviously, Jill went for the strong, masculine types (he liked to count himself among them, for some complicated reason), but he just couldn't picture Jill and Boris as lovers. Rather than comment on that, he said, "I agree with you about Abe--and Cille. I knew Cille in college, but I had a good feeling about Abe as soon as I met him. But, I wondered how much of that was that it is just hard for any American to distrust someone who adopts the persona of Abraham Lincoln."

"Let me tell you something else," Natasha said, grabbing Leonard's arm again, "There is something between Abe and Boris..."

Leonard gave her a questioning look.

"No, not sexual and not even friendly. On the contrary, something bad. Something in past. I...." she released Leonard's arm and hurriedly turned away. Leonard stood numbly, wanting to run after her, as she walked toward the building.

The door opened and Jill and Richard and Boris came out. Leonard quickly turned toward his car and opening the door, released the hood latch. He went and lifted the hood and checked the oil. The sawed off twelve gauge was still safely stowed in the engine compartment. He thought back to the time he dated Virginia in Saginaw whose ex had been stalking her.

Virginia had been afraid of her ex and Leonard had told her, "No matter how tough, I don't know anyone that can take a double load of birdshot at close range and still be a threat." The woman expressed doubt. Fortunately, he never had the chance to prove his assumption. He didn't want to arouse suspicion by taking too long in checking, but there were also two. 357 magnum revolvers hidden there. One was loaded with hollow points, the other with alternating jacketed and solid lead. He closed the hood and pushed down on it to latch it. He decided to finish the show and got the tire gauge out of the glove compartment and checked the tires too. Everything was fine. He wanted people to think he was just fastidious about car care so they wouldn't be suspicious about his checking the concealed guns. He put the tire gauge back and closed the passenger door and walked back toward the building.

The group of three that had come out onto the loading dock were still talking quietly and he nodded as he mounted the steps and they turned toward him. He asked if anyone knew where a car wash was, that the car was pretty dusty from the road trip. No one seemed to know.

Leonard walked into the lunch room and Abe and Cille and Natasha were sitting talking and drinking tea. Natasha excused herself and slid past Leonard, giving him a significant glance. Leonard grabbed a cup of coffee and took her still-warm chair.

"I seem to be the cause of a schism here," he opened. "If I am the cause of a split in the happy family, I can leave, although I think I have a lot to offer...I don't want to ruin what you have worked hard to establish."

Abe and Cille looked at him and at each other. Cille said, "You are welcome here. If someone has a problem with you, I think they can talk to you and work things out. No group is free of conflict. Sometimes conflict is good." A calico cat that had wandered in jumped into her lap and she stroked its fur.

"Well, okay, but..." Leonard had a million thoughts crowding his brain and concluded with, "Okay, thanks."

Abe stood up. "Cille and I are going out for supper in about an hour. Would you like to join us?—I'd like to continue our conversation of this morning."

"Sure; thanks. I seem to have worked up an appetite! We can take my car."

"Meet us at our place in about an hour then," Abe said and walked out.

Cille stayed and seemed to have something on her mind, so Leonard settled back with a warm-up on his coffee. "Leonard," Cille began, "There is a lot going on, and there was a lot going on before you came. You are not the cause of things, maybe more of a seed crystal—you know, like in a cloud how a mote of dust is the seed for water to condense on and make a raindrop. The conditions were all there, and now you have provided the things that seem to suddenly produce…rain."

"Yeah. Okay," Leonard said, "I can see that."

"Well, rain is…rain. Neither good nor bad." She stood up and the cat jumped down. "See you in a bit."

"Yeah, right; I'll be there." Leonard got up and moved so his back wasn't to the door and finished his coffee. He thought of the story by Hemingway, where the soldier comes home and thinks things will be right again, but then everything goes wrong. A cat came in and jumped in his lap. It seemed familiar somehow. Then as it kneaded his lap to settle in, he saw that it had six toes—it was a Hemingway. He knew because his ex-wife's brother had one. Very strange. In college he and Cille called these "sychronicities."

He slowly finished his coffee, then, reluctantly told the cat he had to go and put the cat on the floor. Before he went back upstairs, he went back outside to answer nature's call and the cat followed him. He walked behind the box that he used for a toilet room and the cat played in the weeds. He zipped up, walked to the cat. It rolled over on its back and he bent to scratch its stomach. Something flew over his head and pinged against the metal box—an arrow!

"Hey!" Leonard shouted as he popped up and looked in the direction the arrow had come from.

He saw the three of them standing on the roof of an outbuilding about fifty yards away. Jill was holding a bow and said, "Oh, my gawd, I didn't see you!"

Leonard was reluctant to believe it after all that had happened. "What the hell are you doing!"

"I am so sorry!" Jill said. "We were just target shooting and I didn't see you!"

Leonard calmed down a bit, still not sure what to believe— if it had been Richard or Boris with the bow, he would have had no doubts, but Jill? He couldn't, or didn't want to believe it. "Well, be careful!"

From that distance, he couldn't see their expressions, but felt that Richard and Boris were smirking. They said nothing. Richard grabbed the bow from Jill's hands.

Leonard went to his "room" and made sure no one was around. He took what Natasha said seriously and dug through his belongings and found the palm-sized. 22 semi auto pistol. He checked the load, five high-speed hollow point rounds. He racked one round into the chamber, lowered the hammer, pulled the magazine and replaced the round he'd just chambered so he had six in the gun and snapped the magazine back in place. He put the safety on and stuck the little gun in the waist band of his underwear.

There was a quiet tapping on the door at the stairs. Leonard looked up and Jill slowly opened the door and called, "Leonard, are you there?"

"Yes, over here."

Jill walked part way into the room. "I wanted to tell you how sorry I was about the incident with the bow and arrow."

"That 'incident' could have gotten me dead!" he growled.

"I know, I know," Jill said. "I feel so badly!"

"What the hell were you doing?"

"Well, we were fooling around with the bow and the guys were talking about deer hunting from stands and how we should go up on the roof and try shooting from there. So we went up there. I had shot when we were on the ground and I had hit the target better than they had, so Richard gave me the bow and said, 'Let's see how you do from up here.'"

Leonard's mind was trying to put it all together. "So it was Richard's idea?"

"Well, yeah, but then Boris said, "Bet you can't hit that bush over by the garbage bin in the courtyard. We had been shooting into the woods on the other side of the building we were standing on before that. I am sort of nearsighted and hate to wear glasses, and can't stand to put in contacts, so I didn't see you. Anyway, I was aiming for the base of the bush, but my arrow went high."

"It would seem to go high, people often make that mistake when shooting from a stand…" said Leonard, "they judge the distance based on the length of their line of sight and not the horizontal distance if they and their target were at the same height, so they think the target is further away than it is, so they overshoot."

"I don't get it," said Jill, "but I'm glad for whatever reason that I missed you."

"Me too…But neither Richard nor Boris saw me? They didn't warn you? They can't both be nearsighted too?" asked Leonard.

"No, now that you mention it…But you were behind that bush—I guess they just didn't see you."

"Just a coincidence that they happened to pick as a target the bush I just happened to be standing behind."

"Oh, that is odd, now that you mention it! Especially when we had been shooting in totally the other direction, for the very reason of safety. Again, I have to take the blame because I should have known better."

"But it was Boris who picked out that bush to shoot at, not Richard."

"Well, yes, it was Boris, but I am sure it wasn't intentional! It had to have been a coincidence," Jill said, sounding a little uncertain.

"Jill, I'll tell you something that you may find odd, but it works for me and has kept me alive all these many years—I don't believe in coincidences."

"Then, that means…." Jill looked at him long and hard, "you either don't trust me, or you believe Boris…wanted…."

Leonard made the decision that it wasn't Jill. He hoped he wouldn't regret it—he hoped he might at least live to regret it as he said, "Jill, I see no reason not to trust you." He gave him a hard look. "I hope I am not making a mistake. You have no reason to want me dead…?"

"Oh, God, no!" said Jill, and Leonard saw tears sparkle in Jill's eyes.

Leonard continued, "If there is anything I have done to make you mad at me, I would hope you would discuss it with me, because the fact of the matter is, I like you. Is there anything I have done to you that you are mad at me about? I haven't accidentally killed your turtle or anything?" he said, thinking again of the Clint Eastwood movie.

"Huh?"

"A lame attempt at humor," Leonard said.

"Absolutely not—I mean about no reason to be angry with you. You have been very nice to me. You haven't rejected me for being gay, nor have you wanted to jump my bones," adding parenthetically, "sadly," and continued, "Some people view me as the equivalent of the female 'dumb blond' and just want to use me. Anyway, you have been very straight—I mean you have been up front with everything and…" he took a deep breath and let it out as he said, "I like you too," in a rush.

"I don't mean to pry, but if you could tell me, it might help me, what is your relationship to Boris?"

Jill took another deep breath and let it out, then said, "Boris fancies me. I don't understand it myself. Maybe I am his ideal of the American redhead he wants to possess or conquer or whatever. Sort of the sick thing with different races, black guy wanting a white woman to dominate, or vice versa."

"I understand what you are saying," Leonard said, "Thanks."

He wanted to ask Jill what he knew about Abe and even Richard, but thought he'd grilled him enough. Jill gave him a quick hug and flounced off and out the door.

Leonard looked at his wind up clock and saw it was about time to go upstairs. He made sure the gun was secure and laughed when he thought of Jill hugging him and if he'd felt it.

Jill would be just the one to say, "Is that a gun in your pocket, or are you just glad to see me."

Leonard flounced out of the room and went up the steps to Cille and Abe's place.

Leonard knocked softly on the door of Abe and Cille's "flat" and walked in. Abe zipped over on the Segway. Leonard was thinking that a Segway was a very good idea and if he couldn't get one, roller skates was the next best thing.

"Welcome, Leonardo" said Abe as he dismounted. "Cille will be along in a moment."

"I had an interesting afternoon..." Leonard started.

Abe interrupted, "Well, your morning must have been quite something, and I got to witness some of your noon, so if your afternoon topped those, I'm all ears!"

"It did." Leonard replied, "Yup, I would definitely have to say it did. But lets wait till Cille is here and I don't want to talk here—little pitchers and all that."

"There are children present?" said Abe, looking around, feigning surprise.

"Only emotionally...." said Leonard.

Cille walked over and they made their descent and walked into the courtyard to Leonard's car. No one else seemed to be around. Leonard scanned the nearby rooftops apprehensively.

Abe noticed and said, "Expecting a pigeon to drop by?"

"More likely a hawk," said Leonard. Since he had left the car unlocked, he looked in it before opening the door. Then his paranoia got the better of him and he popped the hood release and looked in the engine compartment. To cover up, he checked the oil again. Everything seemed to be in order. He pushed the hood closed and got in the car. Abe was sitting in front and Cille behind him.

"Everything okay?" asked Abe.

"Well, I was going to tell you it's been burning oil, but that isn't true. Yeah, everything seems to be okay. I'll tell you more about that in a second, but first, which way do I go to get to the place?"

Abe directed him as he drove and Leonard told them about the incident with the arrow.

"Guns aren't allowed on the premises, but we never thought about bows..." Abe said.

"I didn't know about the guns—only in the building?"

"Well, that's a good question. We never thought about it in detail and I guess we never told you." He looked at Cille and she shrugged. "I assume that you do have guns? Wait, don't answer that..." Abe went on, "Why don't you continue with your story and not get into specifics about any weapons you may or may not have for the moment. I think modern Presidents have termed this, 'Don't ask, don't tell.' Well, I'm not asking."

"Okay," Leonard replied. "This is a bit of a problem for several reasons. I believe in the Second Amendment, I believe in the right to self defense by whatever means necessary. And, since I have been threatened, and not only that, the threats seem to possibly have been acted on...I want to make it clear that don't believe that Jill wanted to kill me, but I do think that maybe he was the unwitting agent of Boris and/or Richard.

"Now, I know it would be a mess for you to exempt me, or to change rules now, or whatever. I suppose the simplest way would have been to lie to you, but I don't like to do things that way."

He took a deep breath and continued, "I could always buy a cross bow and I am a fair hand with some other things...It just seems that if you want to kill someone, there are plenty of ways to do it, with or without firearms. I have heard of people being killed with paper cups and pencils, but I have found carrying a crossbow everywhere I go to be a bit inconvenient. Though in college, when I was threatened by some guys in a racial thing, I did carry a steel bed leg with me wherever I went—kept discretely in a plastic pull string bag."

"I can imagine how discrete that was," Abe said dryly.

Cille said, "When was this?"

"Oh, I guess it was sophomore year. It's a long story, but WMU wasn't quite the safe middle class school most everyone seemed to think it was. If you only went to class and stayed in your dorm at night, it was pretty safe. But there were several rapes of women just going between dorms through the food tunnels." He stopped to explain that they called the corridors connecting the dorms to the cafeterias "food tunnels". Abe said he knew about the food tunnels.

He continued, "I, on the other hand, wandered around all hours of the night, was involved in drugs and was often in the wrong place at the wrong time. Surely you remember the Black fraternities, as in para-military units, marching through the cafeteria in uniforms, chanting and then stationing people at the doors and jumping people?"

He looked at Cille in the mirror and she showed only amazement. "You'd think we went to different schools," he continued. "I assure you, these things happened. Anyway, that's off the subject at hand. But, let me tell you some of the things that are going on sub rosa at the mill." He started telling them about what Natasha had told him, but had just started when Abe directed him to turn into the parking lot of the restaurant. The name of the place was "The Fisherman's Wharf."

The lot was almost full and he parked in the back. He considered a full parking lot at a restaurant a good sign and loved seafood, so he was looking forward to the meal as they walked in. The décor was everything one would expect from a restaurant named as it was. The lighting was subdued and the place seemed welcoming and they followed the young lady to one of the few open tables near the back. Neither Abe nor Cille seemed to recognize anyone there, so Leonard thought they could continue their conversation. The waitress brought menus and asked what they wanted to drink. Abe told Leonard that they had several micro-brews and Leonard suggested they get a pitcher of whatever Abe and Cille recommended. Abe ordered an ale called "Amber Waves of Ale" and told Leonard it was better than its name might suggest.

"Just as long as the waves aren't reverse peristaltic waves," quipped Leonard.

They talked small talk until the pitcher came and Abe poured. "I think it's safe to talk here, though there is a pitcher, but it has only one ear."

Cille gave him a puzzled look and then looked expectantly at Leonard. Leonard continued with his story, telling them what Natasha had said to him about Boris. He concluded by telling them that Natasha had said he could trust Abe and since he had instinctively trusted Abe, he felt that made Natasha pretty trustworthy too.

Abe chuckled, "I thank you both for your votes of confidence!" He quaffed his ale and wiped his lips. Suddenly he grew somber, Leonard felt as though he were watching a sunny field when the shadow of a cloud passes over it. "Leonard, you seem to be like a lightning rod—in the two days you have been here, you have had so much happen! Mind you, I'm not blaming you; I'm not saying it's bad, it is just…exceedingly interesting. You are like…"

"A seed crystal?" Leonard said, looking at Cille.

"Exactly!" said Abe, "I couldn't have put it better myself!"

"Well, that's exactly what Cille told me earlier today. Seed crystal, catalyst, lightning rod—that's me." Leonard took a drink and then said, "I hate to bring this up, but Natasha started to mention something about something between you and Boris?"

Cille shifted in her seat and looked pained. Leonard expected her to speak, but she just grabbed her drink and took a big swallow and looked down at the table.

Abe said, "Something between Boris and me? I can't imagine what. We just met, what was it Cille?…a year, maybe a year and a half ago, and while we aren't what I would call fast friends, we have no animosity that I know of. I wonder what she meant?"

"I'll ask her next time I see her. Maybe I misunderstood. As you say, a lot has happened in a very short time. The story of my life. I have been known to get things wrong."

Oh, tell me about that!" said Abe, "just the other day…" Another cloud passed over the field of his face and he stopped. "What were you saying?"

Leonard laughed and looked at Cille before her return look frightened him into silence, but then she laughed too and they all laughed and Leonard poured another round.

The waitress came over with another pitcher. She studied Leonard for a second and said, "I think you know my brother?"

"Oh, I doubt it, Miss, I am new in town—just moved in to the mill where these people are living."

"Exactly; that's what he said!"

"But, Miss, I haven't met anyone here yet, I have only been to town once…" Leonard looked at her more closely…, "Is Raul your brother?"

"Right!" she said excitedly. "He said you were very nice to him. Anyway, this pitcher is free." She plunked it down and started to walk away.

"Wait, Miss!" Leonard said, "Lest there be any misunderstanding, umm, I don't…I'm not…do you know your brother is…?"

She laughed, "A flamer? Well, duh! Kinda hard to miss, wouldn't you say?"

"Well, yeah, but…"

"You're not," she finished for him. "Whether you are or you aren't, you treated Raul nice and he thought that was very nice of you. Anyway, the beer is a token of thanks."

"Thank you, I still don't think I deserve it, but thank you very much." Leonard was trying to think back to what had happened at the other restaurant and what he had said and done—it seemed like weeks ago! He looked at Cille and Abe to see them smiling knowingly.

"Seed crystal…" said Abe sagely and nodded. He looked at Cille who nodded in return. Leonard gulped the last of his beer and topped off all the glasses from the new pitcher. He raised his glass to his lips, half expecting some trick—no smell of bitter almonds anyway!

The rest of the dinner was uneventful, except when Abe excused himself "to see a man about a horse" and Cille said,

"We need to talk about Abe and Boris, but for now, I just want to tell you that Abe has dementia and has lost much of his memory. This seems to have affected long term memory, whereas usually things like Alzheimer's mainly affect short term memory. It seems to get worse at night—known as 'Sundowner's Syndrome.'"

Leonard felt sick. How could this happen to a decent guy like Abe? He thought of all the wonderful people he knew that had been stricken with horrible disease—his own mother having died of cancer. Yet truly evil men went through life unscathed. Pol Pot, Hitler, Stalin, the Huseins—*well, maybe there was hope after all!*

PART II

When they got home, Leonard really wanted to talk to Cille about Abe's past, put there was no opportunity. Cille and Abe invited Leonard up to their flat to talk and have a nightcap. They lit one of the lanterns by the back door and went upstairs. They chatted for a while about the mill and Leonard's ideas. After a while Abe started to nod and Leonard suggested they call it a night.

He was surprised when Abe said, "Leonardo, before you go, maybe you could help me with something. I have some journals, or I guess what you might call diaries, and darned if I can make heads or tails of them. They are written in Cyrillic alphabet and Cille mentioned that you minored in Russian in college. Maybe you could translate them. I am a bit foggy these days and when I do look up words or try to, they don't make sense. Maybe you could peruse them in your spare time--See what you can make of them."

He lit another lantern and left, returning a short time later with an accordion folder. "These appear to be the oldest—the dates are understandable, but nothing else is." He dropped the folder in Leonard's lap. "Well, I'm an old man and need my sleep, so I'm going to bed. Feel free to stay and chat with Cille—maybe she can help you decipher the papers. Two minds are often better than one, but mine is pretty well shot. If nothing else, you two can catch up on old times and don't need me around! See you tomorrow." He bent over and gave Cille a peck on the lips and spun away.

Cille seemed as surprised as Leonard. "He has never let me look at them before!"

Leonard opened the folder and took out the sheaf of papers—all in a crabbed, but legible handwriting. "Who wrote these, do you know?"

"Well, yes, Abe/Robert wrote them. But something has happened to his brain and he can no longer read them—he says he used a code and he cannot remember the key—and it drives him crazy when he thinks about it. He knows there is something very important in them, but can't remember what. I'm glad he entrusted them to you; I wanted you to see them, but didn't feel right about going behind Robert's back."

Leonard put his brandy down and looked at the first page. "My Russian is darn rusty—it's been thirty some years since I took it...." He began to read out loud. "This is not Russian, that's for sure..." He read, 'Toodae ya xad somteeng eenteeresteen...' He and Cille looked at each other—"It's in English!" they said simultaneously.

"Oh, my God," said Cille, "all this time fretting about this and it was so simple!"

"Well," said Leonard, "Puzzles are always simple once you have the key! It's funny; great minds and all that, but I used to do the same thing in my journals when I didn't want anyone to decipher them. My Russian was too rusty to use directly, but most people cannot read Cyrillic, so I just transliterated the English sounds. That's what Abe has done, with a few Russian pronouns left in here and there. But why Russian? Apparently Abe/Robert knew Russian?"

"Well, yeah—he was a poly sci proff at Western. Oh, I guess you never took poly sci. Anyway, he was good and he often brought in "Eezvestia" and "Pravda" and translated articles for the class, then lecturing on them."

"Wait—Abe was your proff in college? That's where you met him?"

"Yeah," I thought I had written you all this.

"Not me."

"Yes, he was magnificent. I had a crush on him, and…well, you see the result."

Leonard felt a twinge of jealousy—that somehow Robert had taken advantage of this naïve coed; but he knew it was a stupid thought. He couldn't think of anyone better for Cille— and certainly not him.

"Well, crap; you know what happened; why are we wasting time reading diaries when you were right there!"

"But I wasn't there until about 1973 and these go back further."

"But still—why don't you start by telling me what you know—like did you ever meet or see Boris back then? Do you know why Abe would even have known someone like Boris? And, for that matter, who is Boris? What was he to Abe? And lastly, what happened to Abe? Did he have a stroke or get Alzheimer's or what—Christ, Cille, you were with him, what the hell happened!?"

Cile replied, "I don't know anything about Boris; as far as I know I have never seen Boris until he came here with Natasha-Theomina. I was leery of both of them, though I have grown to feel okay about Natasha. But I never felt good about Boris and still don't, but Abe accepted them both—you know Abe."

"Apparently I don't know Abe. Turns out that this all-American icon speaks, or spoke fluent Russian and had Russian friends. I know very little about Abe. Is he from the Soviet Union—Russia? He certainly has no accent that I can discern."

"He told me that he learned Russian in the army and I assumed he meant the United States Army. I always had the inkling that he had been in army intelligence, but never pursued it and Robert didn't talk about his past. He did say that both parents were dead, died when he was a kid."

"Too bad we don't have computer access—maybe we could find something through the internet, though I have never used it for that and am not sure how you go about that…" Leonard interjected.

"We could go to the library in town—they have computers with net access."

"Okay, something we can do this coming week. Anyway, the important thing right now is what happened to Robert to affect his mind, his memory, so badly? Did this happen suddenly or what?"

"I don't really know—we were together while I was in college and everything was fine. Then after I graduated, Robert urged me to go to grad school, but we felt that there were better schools for graduate studies, especially to get an MSW…"

"MSW?" Leonard interrupted.

"Yeah, masters in social work. It was a big decision, obviously, but Robert insisted, said I'd be wasting my talent if I didn't do it and maybe it'd give me some space to really fly (is how he put it). Almost, in retrospect, like he wanted to have me away from him. He was so sweet, I thought he had my best interests at heart, but after I moved, I wondered if he just didn't want me away because he was tired of me—for all I knew, he took up with a different coed every couple years." Cille picked up her glass and drank. "But he had told me he wanted to retire, and we began talking about the future together once I got my masters."

"So you definitely kept in touch during this time?" Leonard asked.

"Oh, yes, we talked on the phone every night. Ran up some pretty big phone bills. And wrote constantly."

"Yeah, back before email…" Leonard mused out loud.

"Yeah, Robert seemed real stoked about retiring—I questioned that, because teaching was his life, but he said he was tired of it all, all the politics, there seemed to be an undercurrent of something else though—almost fear—like it was dangerous to stay. I really can't put my finger on it, especially after all these years, but at the time I definitely felt that he had a tangible fear of something associated with his work."

"Hmmm…" murmured Leonard, "You know what it sounds like to me? Okay, bearing in mind that I am paranoid, but I wonder if he didn't have another 'job,' a profession that Boris was a part of. It almost fits too neatly, but what if, and I know this sounds crazy, but it fits—what if Robert was a spy? What if Boris was a contact, or his handler? (although Boris seems to be too young to be Robert's handler)."

"I don't know…" said Cille, "It sort of fits, but it's hard to imagine Robert as a spy, especially one that would associate with the likes of Boris."

"Well, I imagine that when one is a spy, one doesn't have much choice about with whom one associates. I imagine there are even more unsavory characters than Boris, although right now he strikes me as pretty smelly," Leonard added, thinking of recent incidents. "Okay, so what changed? Something had to have changed. You maybe weren't right there, but…"

"Yes, we were making plans for the future…and it got to where it was a month or so until I graduated and I was looking forward to moving back and it was like Robert suddenly got cold feet. He suggested I wait till the end of summer. He was very vague—something about tying up loose ends before fall and I thought he was talking about his teaching and getting ready to retire.

"But something was definitely bothering him. I told him I wanted to at least come back to see him and why couldn't I help him tie things up and he was adamant about me staying where I was. I would have suspected there was another woman, but this was even more…" she struggled to find words and took another sip of her drink. "I don't know, just something dangerous…"

"Okay, here's my paranoid fantasy kicking in," said Leonard, swallowing another sip of brandy and pouring another shot, "It sounds as though he wanted to retire, but from the spy game. I know, it sounds crazy, but it fits so well—maybe too well, maybe because my brain is wanting it to fit, but anyway…" he took another slurp of his drink, "but maybe he wanted to retire, but his handlers didn't want him to. Imagine all the effort that went into setting him up and getting him established in place as a sleeper, and now he wants out.

"Well," he said, waving the sheaf of papers, "this may confirm that, though if I were a spy, I don't think I'd be writing about it even in a coded journal. Unless…" Leonard thought for a second, "he was writing this as insurance—send it off or hide it and maybe use it as leverage later—like 'look, leave me out of this or I expose the whole thing'. Wow, very dangerous, if that's what he was doing.…"

Leonard shook his head as he gulped another mouthful of his drink—"But again, this could just be all my paranoid fantasy, fueled by this very smooth brandy I've been drinking way too much of." He looked around, "Umm, I have to use the 'facilities'—I assume the drain is in the corner, same as on my floor?"

Cille nodded and he climbed to his feet and handed her the papers and walked unsteadily to the corner.

When he returned, he asked, "So, did you see Abe, Robert, that summer? You obviously got back together with him...."

"No, I didn't see him that summer. He called and told me something had come up—his brother in Oregon was ill and he had to go out and take care of him and help run his business— he had some import/export business or something. He said everything was a mess and he'd be very busy and didn't know how often he could call or write. It seemed very mysterious, but I didn't know what to do. I offered to go out there with him and he made all sort of excuses why I couldn't and he had to handle it alone. He actually got pretty brusque and so I just left it like that. I wavered between believing him and thinking this was just his way of brushing me off, though I didn't want to believe it."

"So, that's the summer I met you at your parents' house in Pittsburgh while they were away on vacation?"

Cille nodded silently.

"Holy crap, no wonder you were so...distant."

She nodded again.

"Well, at least that explains something to me that I've wondered about and kicked myself over for nigh unto thirty years! Holy..." Leonard didn't know whether to laugh or be angry or cry. The story of his relationship with women.

"I'm sorry," Cille whispered, "but what could I have said? I don't know what was happening myself. I needed a friend and you were that…"

"Yeah, good old Leonard; always there…" He suddenly had the terrible feeling that yes, indeed, and he was still in that role. "So, is that why I am here now?"

A tear trickled down Cille's face, "I'd be lying if I said I didn't need you as a friend right now. I guess I have been selfish—I just didn't know who else. Leonardo, I…"

"I guess I should be flattered that I am seen as being so reliable. Good old sturdy Leonardo. Like a good draft horse, you can really count on him to pull your fat out of the fire. Crap."

Cille looked at him, "It's not like that!" She sobbed, "You always knew how to hurt me the most…

Leonard found himself holding her. "Crap, crap, crap."

Cille pulled away and looked into his face, "Yes, you are reliable. You are a good man. You are the only one I can trust. That says a lot about you—all good. But we were never meant to be lovers. You are a true friend, and that is worth a lot—maybe not to you…"

"I'm here, aren't I?" Even Leonard wasn't exactly sure what he meant by that. "And I'll be here until this is settled." He thought, why change his life strategy now—he knew no other way of being. The seed, the catalyst, the pivot point. Like the Earth's axis.

He pulled away and sat back down, wiping his face and taking another swallow of his drink. "Okay, back to business. So, you did get back together—when?"

"It was after Christmas, after my divorce. One day there was literally a knock on the door, and there was Robert—or in this case, I really should say 'Abe.' He had changed so much—not just appearance, but demeanor, everything. He was a changed man—but in a way, for the better. He was at peace."

"A frontal lobotomy will do that." Leonard said, offhandedly and regretted it. He quickly added, "So, something dramatic happened that fall, and I guess we won't know what until we look into these papers."

"But these are from the sixties—that won't tell us anything," said Cille, flipping through them. Leonard had seen that the dates were in numbers only.

"Yeah, I suppose, other than supplying background. They may tell us why he wanted to leave or who was involved, but I almost am afraid to know." He thought for a minute, "But even if he was writing when this change occurred, would he write about it—would he even be able to write about it?"

"Oh, good, point, I hadn't thought about that. If he changed so dramatically that he was no longer Robert, had a totally different persona, and, possibly, no longer could even read Russian, how could he write about it?" Cille asked.

"But there must have been a core—the inner Robert that you had fallen in love with; wasn't that still there?" asked Leonard.

"I'm not sure…I remember at first feeling that I was seeing him only so I could delve back into him and bring back the real Robert—to in fact find the man I had loved. And I did it because I loved him—sort of the 'for better, for worse.' But then, I found myself falling in love with the new guy. You have to admit, Abe is very likeable. And, it's not like Robert isn't still there…"

"Wow. If any of this is true…I mean, we know that Robert had some 'issues' and suddenly these seem to have resolved themselves and obviously he changed dramatically. That much is true for certain. Maybe he had a nervous breakdown. Maybe this spy stuff is a figment of my fevered imagination…"

"But, there's Boris…"

"Yes," Leonard agreed, "I was just going to say that—there is Boris…Like gum on the bottom of a shoe—or something more smelly…But, we really only know that from what Natasha told me. I am such a poor judge of character—especially when it comes to women."

"I disagree. You are a good judge of character."

"Well, what do you think? Is Natasha trustworthy, or maybe she's the spy master…" said Leonard.

"If she were evil, why would she warn you? And if she is involved, somehow, we are back to accepting the first premise—that Abe was indeed a spy. Whether he knew Boris or Natasha, it seems that would make him a spy—if either one of them are. If they aren't, why would Natasha hint about some mysterious connection from the past? I doubt that Boris or Natasha were Robert's pool cleaners. And there is the fact of Boris having Jill shoot at you with the arrow."

"If I believe that Jill wasn't trying to kill me for his own nefarious reasons. I hate to keep bringing up movies, but this is like 'A Wonderful Mind,' where Nash hallucinates the spies and doesn't know what's real. I'm beginning to wonder—will I wake up tomorrow and be back in my bed in Midland, or for all I know, Pittsburgh, or Kalamazoo. Maybe it is still 1973."

"You have a good imagination, but do you think you could invent thirty years of memories, complete with computers and the internet. You are no Al Gore!"

Leonard laughed, "Well, thank you for that! But I guess you are right. Not even I could come up with such an elaborate fantasy. Plus, you have aged. Hate to say it, but while you aged gracefully, you still have aged, and that was what tipped Nash off that his little girl was a hallucination…Of course, knowing that, I could have aged you in my mind…"

"I don't think so. Would you have imagined that I had to have a crown put on this tooth?" She opened her mouth and pointed to a tooth. "Or that I had an emergency appendectomy?"—she lifted her blouse and pulled the waste band down on her skirt and panties and showed him the scar.

"Or that your doing that would give me such an instant hard on…" He added, "Sorry, but you still do it to me!" She blushed and put her clothes back in order.

Leonard began looking through the papers again. "Even though we now know the key to these, it's still going to take time to plow through them. You say Robert no longer remembers Russian? I was thinking if he just read the sounds out loud, we could all get the meaning together—between the handwriting and my uncertainty about the alphabet anymore, this could take a lot of time." He looked at Cille, "Now, Natasha mentioned that Boris and Abe had a history, but would Boris be in here? I'm wondering if he went by the same name? Let me just look here, Boris should be easy to spot if it's here, or maybe his last name—what was it again?"

"Medelius," Cille replied.

"Right, so a capital 'B' or a capital 'M'." He saw Cille looking over his shoulder and he handed her the bottom half of the sheaf. "Be easier for you if you have your own stack to look at. A Russian 'B' looks like—do you have a pencil?"

She rummaged in her purse and came up with a pen.

Leonard wrote the letter on the folder—"But wait, lets see an example in Abe's own handwriting. Oh, and the 'M' is pretty much the same as in English. Let me write the names 'Boris' and 'Medelius' for you…" He wrote what looked like 'dopuc' and 'Mege^i-oc.' "But let's see if we can find…" Leonard flipped through a page or two. "Okay, here's a capital 'b' …" He stopped and looked more carefully at where his finger was pointing, "Damn, there it is right there, Boris, unless I'm mistaken."

"What's it say?"

Leonard plowed through the language, sounding it out slowly and Cille repeated it in regular sounding English to come up with, "My *tovarisch*, Boris, came over to the house today…" Leonard stopped, "Now, Robert used the Russian here, *tovarisch,* and that can mean friend, but it can also mean…and at the time this was written it would have a meaning…more like a comrade—sort of military. But I may be reading too much into it."

They began reading references to Boris out loud to each other. It appeared that Robert knew Boris quite well and didn't like him very much. Boris was apparently Robert's "handler" and he resented that for many reasons, chief among them was that Boris was young and arrogant.

After several minutes of reading and deciphering, Leonard said, "Okay, so we know how Boris and Abe know each other, and some inkling of friction between them. If we want to know how it unfolded, it's going to take months of reading—reading files more recent than this one. I just don't see us being able to find much out—and even if we did, what are we going to be able to do with the information? We have to find someone we, and Abe, can trust to turn these over to. I don't know who that would be. The only thing good about these is that if Boris suspects they exist, he may be reluctant to act for fear of the files falling into the wrong hands. He probably is trying to find them, but it seems odd that he hasn't found them before this—or just set the whole place on fi…"

"...on fire?" Cille said, completing his thought.

"So maybe the fire the other day wasn't an accident after all—but..." Leonard stopped—*there was Jill right there in the middle again. Either he was the most unlucky guy, or he wasn't so unwitting after all. And, as Leonard said before, he didn't believe in coincidences. Still, Jill would make a pretty good fall guy—sort of the dumb blond, easily led. Except he had seen a glimmer of his rapier wit in the restaurant—but maybe he was only capable of verbal sparring...* "I've got to think this all over. I'm soo confused!" he said with mock exasperation, only the mock part wasn't so mock.

Leonard continued, "Well, I think we have gone as far as we can, no pun intended, tonight. Tomorrow's Sunday, lets get together again and go over these papers—maybe Abe can find some that are more recent. Do you know where he keeps them?"

"Oh, good question—no, I don't."

"Well, I'll take these for safe keeping until I can see him again. And I may try to talk to Natasha about what she knows about Abe's relationship with Boris." He stood up. "I'd better get to my flat while I can still walk! Good night, Cille." He bent to kiss her and she handed him the folder. "Oh, is any of Abe's hangover cure around—I think I'll need it!"

Cille mixed something into a glass of water and told him to drink it down. She pecked him on the cheek and he went down to his flat. Leonard thought he heard steps on the stairs below him, but couldn't be sure. He was glad he hadn't lit the lantern. He took his shoes off and tied them around his neck. He returned it to the ground floor and then walked back up to his floor. He got to his room, threw the file under some of his own journals in a box in the corner, threw the his shoes on top and fell into bed, stopping to take the pistol out of his waistband and place it under his pillow.

The next morning he woke up feeling surprisingly good and looked at his clock. It was a little before nine. He remembered it was about one when he went to bed. He was hungry. He decided to go out again to eat, and thought he would run out of money pretty quickly if he continued eating so many meals out and vowed to go to get some groceries when he'd had breakfast. He assumed that there was a communal refrigerator—though he wondered because there seemed to be no electricity.

Leonard changed out of the clothes he'd worn to bed and replaced the pistol. He went downstairs. No one appeared to be up yet. But when he got to his car, Natasha hurried out of the building and came over to him. "Are you going into town?" she asked.

"Yes, you want a ride? Hop in." He hoped he could get away before anyone else joined them so he could talk with her in private.

They got in the car and he drove out of the compound. "I was hoping to talk to you alone and ask you about what you had said about Abe and Boris having known each other from before," Leonard began, unable to beat around the bush with small talk.

"That's about all I know—just that they knew one another. Boris doesn't talk much about what he does, but he did mention he had met Abe before or knew him in the past. Very vague. I think Boris is up to something bad—he is criminal or something. But Abe does not seem like bad man, so I don't understand this."

"Will Boris be suspicious of you leaving with me?"

"I told him I needed to buy more food, which I do, and I would see if I could get ride with you. He seemed unconcerned."

"Okay. That's good. Oh, speaking of food, is there like a refrigerator in the kitchen we can all use, or what?"

"There is a refrigerator that runs on bottled gas. You can use—but people tend to share even things they did not buy themselves…"

Leonard thought that was a nice way to put that some people were moochers. "I would like to stop and eat breakfast—I can drop you somewhere and pick you up when I'm finished, or, what I'd like better, would be for you to join me—if we can find someplace that you would be okay with to eat." Leonard marveled at his twisted syntax, either Natasha's way of speaking was rubbing off on him, or he was just not hitting on all mental cylinders this morning—more likely the latter.

"'Tony's' is good. Has not too bad food—food there is not too unhealthy. I usually don't eat big breakfast, but I can have tea and scones or something like that."

"Fine," said Leonard. "Then I too need to go grocery shopping, if you know a good market, I'll go there with you."

"Very good. Maybe I can influence you to eat better."

"Maybe…" Leonard said, with considerable doubt.

He had hoped to see Raul, to thank him for the pitcher last night, but Raul was not there this morning. Maybe they tried harder to be socially acceptable on Sundays, as there was a cute young lady as their waitress.

When Leonard had a cup of hot coffee and Natasha had settled in with her lukewarm dishwater tea, Leonard asked her if she had known Boris when he was in Kalamazoo in Michigan.

She raised her eyebrows, seemingly surprised that he knew. "Yes, when I first came to this country, we live in Kalamazoo. Did you know there is quite a Russian community there— Jewish."

"No, I didn't know that."

"Yes. Well, Boris came to country and it was arranged for him to marry me. I was student at Kalamazoo College. I was in engineering program. Boris was already engineer, but he went to Western and took classes, mostly to learn English for engineering expressions he already knew."

"Okay. Makes sense. Did he know Abe from going to Western then?"

"I don't know—was Abe a student too? I don't remember Abe as a friend or dropping by to see Boris."

"I believe that Abe was a professor at Western—went by the name 'Robert' then. I don't know what he went by for a last name—maybe same as now?"

"Robert Goldman? Doesn't ring bell."

"But you told me there was something between Boris and Abe; something in the past. So how did you know—what was it in their past?" asked Leonard, becoming impatient. "You sounded concerned, like they were enemies or something." Leonard was doubting his sanity, half expecting her to say, 'I said this?'

"Oh, yes, Boris knew *Abe* in past."

"Are you sure it was that name, not that he had known the man who now calls himself 'Abe'?"

"Oh…I see what you are saying. Boris said, when we moved into mill, that he knew Abe from old country."

"But…are you sure?"

"I am sure that is what Boris said, though he only said it once and sort of as joke—like 'I knew Abe when he was Comrade Starshy Leeyutenant.'"

"Senior Lieutenant…? Asked Leonard.

"Yes. I thought nothing of it—a joke, but…"

"He used those words, *'Starshy Leeutenant' –pa Rooskie, nye Angliski!? Own skazal etot pa Rooski?*" Leonard was emphatic, asking her in Russian whether Boris had said "Senior Lieutenant" **in Russian, not English—he said it in Russian?**

"*Da!*" Natasha answered without thinking.

"Well, that would certainly, at least in my mind, rule out that Abe had been like a Lieutenant in the United States Army. And certainly Boris Medelius was not in the United States Army."

"Certainly not."

"Wow, this certainly puts a whole new complexion on things. Or as Daffy Duck would say, 'What a revolting development!'" He studied Natasha as she drank her tea.

The waitress came and took their orders. Natasha ordered a cherry scone and Leonard ordered eggs over medium, sausage, hash browns and whole wheat toast.

Natasha shook her head, "The only good thing on your plate will be toast."

Leonard winked at her, "The other gives me stamina."

"In that case, eat up," Natasha said enigmatically.

While Leonard was still trying to figure that one out, Natasha said, "I don't think you should get involved in this thing between Boris and Abe. Boris is very dangerous—he enjoys hurting people, this I know. We must trust that Abe can handle things."

"But Abe cannot handle things," Leonard said, "Abe has suffered some disease or something—he has lost most of his memory and has completely changed from the old times when he knew Boris. I really think they were spies or something and Abe suffered some trauma or stroke or something and totally forgot his 'mission'—why he was sent over here…"

Natasha interrupted him, "You know, back in those days, drug culture was very strong. Boris told me about a drug that was supposed to erase memory, but it was experimental. They were not sure memory loss would be permanent."

"Maybe that's why Boris is here—to tie up loose ends and eliminate Abe." Saying it out loud sounded crazy and he expected Natasha to say so.

Natasha just nodded. "I fear that you are correct in what you are thinking. But how can you, or anyone, help Abe?"

"Good question. I am no spy; I don't have any training. I know a little martial arts, but nothing like someone in *Spesnas* might know."

"You are lover, not fighter. This I know."

Leonard laughed.

"No, I tell you truth. You are!"

"Well, you bring out the best in me! The truth is; I do hate violence, now. I used to hunt and loved to kill animals, but now that Dad is gone, I rarely go hunting. I have watched big bucks walk past me. I can't bring myself to shoot. But to protect Abe…I don't know. I had hoped to get through this life without having to do more killing."

"You are not a killer. You are shepherd. You protect the sheep, the innocents."

The waitress brought the food and Leonard's appetite returned when he saw it.

After the waitress left, Natasha nibbled on her scone and looked at Leonard, "You are a fair, decent man. You play fair. But Boris does not. You cannot fight a fair fight with Boris and win. Remember this. If you must fight, you must somehow have an unfair advantage because Boris is well trained. He enjoys hurting people. But also, he will be very hard to surprise, as you say, 'he sleeps with one eye open'. I think you should take Abe and hide."

"Where would you hide someone like Abe? And, I think that's what Abe already tried by coming to this out of the way place. But Boris found him. No, we can't hide Abe. I wish we could, believe me, if there was a way. Boris won't rest until Abe is dead. He can already see; I mean, Boris is a perceptive person, he can see that Abe is harmless now. Yet, I feel that he won't let Abe be."

They ate in silence for a few moments. Leonard said, "You know, in movies they get out of this by having Abe fake his own death, but in reality I think that would be almost impossible. In movies they always have some drug that makes the guy seem dead, or there's a fiery car crash. But even that, I'm afraid, would not fool Boris. There'd have to be a real body of some sort, and those are hard to come by. Don't just go to the market and pick up a dead body. 'One dead body to go, hold the onions.'"

Natasha eyed him. "I think you are just being silly."

"No, not me!" Leonard wanted to be silly; he wanted it all to go away and to have the privilege of just being silly, instead he felt crushing responsibility. Then he said, "Are you in danger from Boris?"

"Not really, at least not at the moment. I think he needs me as part of his cover. But if he accomplishes his mission, who knows? I fear then for everyone, because he will have to leave no ends untied."

"Uh, yeah…. My only question is, why hasn't he killed Abe before this—he's been at the mill for what, a year and a half and has done nothing?"

"He may be tying more loose ends. He has been searching for something, so maybe until he finds whatever it is, we are all safe."

"Man, I'd like to turn this over to the authorities—but who? Who would believe it? 'Well, you see, Boris and Natasha have come here from Russia and Mr. Big is giving Boris instructions and Boris is going to kill Abe Lincoln…' Yeah, I can see it, then they say 'Sure, sure buddy, you don't get yourself all worked up, we will take care of it, here, try on this nice white coat, let me tie it for you, it laces up in back. Oh, Bruno, we need the shot of chlorpromazine over here.'"

They finished and Leonard paid the bill. Natasha insisted on paying her share. On the way back she directed him to a little market with lots of produce and organically grown food. Leonard even found some things he could eat. He splurged and bought a six pack of Coke, much to Natasha's chagrin. She said, "Do you know that if you put Coca Cola on automobile, it take the paint off?"

"So would my stomach acid," Leonard said, but added, "Point taken—it is bad for teeth."

They loaded the groceries in the trunk of the car. Leonard took the opportunity to gather the sawed off shotgun and one of the pistols and put them into a cardboard box so he could take them up to his room—rules or not, as Natasha said, playing by the rules was a good way to get dead in this case.

When they got back, they unloaded their stuff. No one was around, so Leonard suggested they walk down by the river. When they were in a secluded spot, as if on signal they shed their clothes and made fast, furious love. He didn't even care if they were seen together as the returned to the mill—what would Boris do, kill him?

When they walked into the building, Abe and Cille were eating breakfast and invited Leonard and Natasha.

Natasha declined and left.

Leonard said, "I just ate. But I would like to talk to you about last night and go over some things. Can I meet you in your flat later—maybe in an hour?"

They agreed and Leonard went up to the top roof to shower. When he got up there, Natasha was there, apparently with the same idea. They showered together and made love again. When they were through, Natasha said, "Maybe I should stop criticizing what you eat—if this is what it does for you—you said it helps stamina?"

"I like to think so."

She swatted him with her towel and got dressed and left.

Leonard went down to his place and got the file folder, then went up to the top roof. Maybe a different perspective, more open vitas, or something, anything, might help. Besides, he wanted to see the path of the old flume and where the mill pond was in relationship to the building from a bird's eye view and walked over to the edge of the roof. He thought he'd have a better view from the elevator penthouse and went over and climbed up the outside ladder to its roof. He was a little concerned with being close to the edge, as the wind was blowing pretty hard, so he sat down. It was too windy to look through the papers, so he was just looking toward the ravine when he heard voices. It sounded like Boris and Richard on the roof below, though he couldn't see them. The wind was blowing their voices to him and he could hear them quite well.

Boris' voice, "I reactivated…now that Leonard is here, more seems to be happening…Robert gave him some diaries…I know, but his belongings are all in one place and something of Robert's may look out of place…Search when he's gone."

Richard's voice, "I suppose I could arrive a little late…Don't know what I'm looking for."

Boris voice came back, "…there's still fire…make sure it works this time…we know it is here…One of them has it."

They must have moved because Leonard didn't hear any more. He waited, not sure if they had left. He was still for what seemed like an eternity, but he figured it was ten minutes at the most. Hearing nothing more, he slowly rose to a crouch and looked around. He carefully inched his way toward the ladder. He crawled to the edge there and looked down. Not seeing them, he started down the ladder. Once down he figured he'd pretend he had gone up there to get some sun and fell asleep if they were still there—he couldn't stay up there forever. He walked casually around the corner and over to the doorway to go back down. The roof was clear.

Leonard had to hide the folder. Leonard wondered about how Boris and Richard knew he'd be gone and what that had to do with one of them arriving late—then he remembered the group was meeting that night to discuss plans for winter and such. So, it sounded like Richard would be looking for Abe's papers in Leonard's things while Leonard was at the meeting.

Boris must have planted a bug in Abe and Cille's flat and overheard them talking with Leonard last night. He wondered how many other places were bugged. He figured they had limited manpower for listening to the bugs, or tapes, so maybe that's all they had gotten so far.

But he had to move the papers—and the guns! He hoped they didn't know about them.

Leonard thought how ironic it would be for him to hide the folder in with Boris's stuff, but thought that Boris most likely had some sort of surveillance on his flat. Same with Richard and Jill. But that gave him an idea—Richard and Jill had sort of taken over control of the fourth floor storage area too. He hoped they wouldn't have bugged it—seemed like they could only spread their resources so thin. He didn't have a lot of time to fool around.

He decided too, that they would not stop looking till they found something, so he leafed through and found pages without any reference to Boris. He feared he was leaving in too much good stuff, and could only read them so fast. He picked out several that said a lot of nothing and put them together and stuck them in the folder. He stuck the folder under his mattress. He put the rest of the journal into a plastic bag and taped it with duct tape and threw it into the cardboard box with the guns. He tossed some of the groceries he'd bought into the box on top of the other things.

He went down the stairs with the box, hoping he wouldn't encounter anyone along the way. He stopped and listened at fourth floor and hearing nothing, went in. He left the box near the door and took the manuscript and put it in the barrel where the oily rags had burned Not the best hiding place, but okay for now. He made sure that he hadn't left any visible prints in the dust and walked back into the stair well with his box of goodies.

He saw through the wall of windows that no one was in the lunchroom area, so he walked through and listened. No one seemed to be in the adjoining kitchen either, so he walked through the open doorway and stuck the box on the counter behind the door where it wasn't seen immediately as one entered. He was less pleased with that, but didn't have a better idea. He took one of the revolvers out, the one loaded with hollow points, and wrapped it a jacket. He decided to carry that later.

He saw by a clock in the kitchen that it was about four o'clock. He went back to his flat, sat for a moment and had an idea. Many times in the past he had gone with the idea of not fighting and giving in—this strategy worked in self defense and it worked in other areas of life too. One of his tai chi students for months fretted and worried about her house—she was struggling to keep it and every time she saw Leonard, she asked him for advice on how she could keep her house. She said that her grown kids really wanted her to keep it, but they were no longer living there, having married and left, but, of course, none of them could help pay for the house or maintain it. Finally, after wracking his brain, Leonard said, "Look, why are you wanting so badly to keep a house you can't afford, can't maintain, don't particularly like just for your ungrateful kids. Why don't you sell it and move to a place you can afford and more easily maintain—maybe an apartment." So she did and was very happy.

So, if Boris wanted so desperately to have this evidence of Abe's, why not give it to him? Abe seemed beyond caring anymore. The only thing to be careful of was whether the hidden evidence was the only reason that Boris and Richard hadn't killed Abe. But if things kept on their current course, more people might be hurt or killed. The fire may have been set deliberately to burn up the evidence. Maybe there was some way to give Boris the evidence, but sort of fake evidence—the way he had considered and rejected the idea of giving Boris a dead body, burned beyond recognition and letting him believe it was Abe. Leonard even thought of somehow making Boris believe that when the oily rags had burned, they had already burned the manuscript, but if Boris had actually set the fire, he would know that wasn't true.

Leonard didn't believe even giving Boris the real papers would stop him—he would probably kill everyone involved. But what if Boris thought that Leonard was a pragmatic type that would even consider trading away Abe's life to protect others, and himself? It may at least buy time. Or, it could be bait for a trap. He would have liked to bait the trap and have the FBI or Homeland Security be there to catch Boris, but he felt he didn't have enough time to set it all up. Things were moving to a climax and he just didn't think a call to some government bureaucrat would bring the necessary results. As he had told Natasha, they would probably think he was a crank and ignore him.

Leonard took a pad of paper and wrote in clear letters— "Your place is bugged, we cannot talk here," and hoped he didn't need to explain. He went up to Abe and Cille's floor and knocked on their door. Abe answered after a short wait.

"I hope you are feeling better," Leonard said and showed him the note.

Abe looked at him and said, "Much better, thank you. Maybe I overdid the drinking last night. Cille and I were going for a little walk before dinner, would you care to join us?"

He went to where Cille was sitting and tapped her on the shoulder and showed her the note, then said to her "Cille, Leonard would like to join us for our walk, is that okay?"

"Sure; that would be nice."

"It's a beautiful day. Maybe work up an appetite before dinner and talk about my ideas for a flume," Leonard said as they left.

They were silent until they got into the courtyard. Even then Leonard stuck with small talk. "Let's take my car and go to the park and we can walk there."

They got in the car and he showed them the note again and pointed to the inside of the car and mimed that he wasn't sure. They chatted about the fine day and inconsequential stuff until they got to the mill pond park. Leonard parked the car and when they were away from it, he said, "I may be overly cautious, but I overheard Boris and Richard and they mentioned they had a listening device in your flat. I didn't know where else they may have concealed bugs, including my car. I just hope they don't have one hidden on our clothing or something." He had always heard that running water defeated bugs, and even though he doubted it was true any more, he walked them over to the falls and against that backdrop told them everything he knew and concluded with his idea to give them at least part of Abe's diaries.

They talked for a while. Abe was excited to learn that Leonard and Cille had cracked his "code" and laughed at how simple it was. He marveled that he couldn't have remembered it.

Leonard told them that he was afraid that even if they gave Boris what he wanted, he would not be satisfied and would probably still kill Abe and probably just about everyone else to make sure there were no loose ends. He told about his desire to turn everything over to the FBI or Homeland Security, but mentioned his doubts.

Abe laughed. "The FBI is already involved!" he said.

Leonard and Cille looked at him, "What?!" they said together.

"Oh, yeah," Abe replied. "A year or so ago, I contacted my old friend, Morris. I started remembering things and after I retired, we had kept in touch—mostly Christmas cards and the like. I told him that I was afraid I was in trouble. You know, when people get Alzheimer's, they start to forget things..."

Cille and Leonard nodded, knowingly.

"Well, it was the reverse—I started remembering things. I hadn't even remembered who Morris was for several years, and then I was going through some stuff getting ready to move and I found cards from him and it all came back—well, not all, but a bit. So I took considerable effort and located him. Almost simultaneously with my 'reawakening,' Boris showed up. Sort of at the periphery, if you know what I mean. At least at first. Then he seemed emboldened. Cille and I had moved out here and then we heard about the mill. Well, we sort of put feelers out for people to help us with a sort of 'urban homesteading' project and one of the first to show up were Boris and Natasha. As soon as I saw them again, it triggered a flood of memories. I even remembered where I had my journals, but couldn't read them. (Ingenious, your discovering all I had to do was read them out loud!)."

Leonard didn't want to interrupt for fear of cutting Abe's delicate thread, but did interject, "So, who is this FBI guy? Can we get him here?"

"Oh, he's already here—you know, *Morris.*"

"Morris? I know him?"

"Good grief, man, who is suffering the memory deficit here? Morris--Morrie"

"That Morrie?!" Leonard was flabbergasted—"Are you sure? I mean...I don't mean..."

"You mean, you don't mean?" Abe laughed, "You're sounding like Richard Nixon. Or Bill Clinton. Maybe John Kerry..."

"I don't mean to doubt you, but this is pretty important. Morrie that lives at the mill, is an FBI agent?"

"Retired, but still...he is forwarding information to them."

"I hate to be...to doubt you, but, considering everything, you are absolutely certain this isn't a fantasy?"

"I am certain," said Abe.

"As certain as your name is Abraham Lincoln," said Leonard.

"Exactly!" Abe exclaimed.

Leonard's heart stopped and he and Cille looked at each other in alarm.

Abe laughed, "Come on! I'm joshing you! I know I am Robert Goldman, although that also is just a nom la guerre."

Leonard was no longer sure of anything. "You aren't helping my confidence. Who the hell is Richard Corey then— and please, no jokes."

"That, I m not sure of," replied Abe. "I'm thinking he is either Boris's handler, or his assistant, but I am pretty sure they are associates."

"What about Jill?" asked Leonard.

"Jill is an unknown quantity, as is Tom. Jill arrived right after Richard and they immediately took up together."

"What about Liv?" Cille asked.

"She and Tom showed up together at the same time as Richard and Jill and were locals, and I assumed they knew each other from living around here," answered Abe.

"Well," continued Leonard, "We should be getting back for dinner. But, if it's okay with you, I will give them the somewhat sanitized package and see what happens. If we can get Morrie involved with springing the trap, so much the better. But I just think this has to happen right away—maybe even tonight. Can you tell him our plan?"

"Yes, I'll take him aside after dinner," said Abe.

As they started back to the car, Leonard physically pulled Cille aside and said, "Is what Abe says about Morrie true? You know him—is this just some delusion…?"

"I don't know. I don't know. It seems too…pat to be real, don't you think? I mean, it is just too terribly convenient to all of a sudden hear that this unlikely person could be a government agent. If we had more time!"

"But we don't," sighed Leonard. "As Julius Caesar said, *'Alias jactet est!' 'The die is cast!'"* Then he added, "But I am trusting more in my guns than in some *deus ex machina.*"

They got back to the mill in time for Cille to run in and help prepare dinner. Normally, Leonard would have helped, but he had a lot on his mind and felt that excused him. The first thing he did was to get the folder from under his mattress and brought it to the kitchen and placed it in the box under the groceries, he reluctantly put the revolver in the coat next to the box. Having second thoughts, he ran back upstairs, found his big sheath knife and tied it on a lanyard around his neck and under his shirt.

All through dinner, every time he looked at someone or talked to them, Leonard found himself weighing them and wondering just who they really were. He doubted everyone and everything, taking nothing at face value. He still could not see pudgy Morrie as FBI. He wanted to pull each person aside for a private conversation, but what would he say? *Hey, are you with the FBI, or is Abe delusional...? Are you really a dangerous spy, or am I just hallucinating?*

After dinner while people were milling around before the meeting, Leonard asked Boris if he could talk to him for a minute. He told him he had found something that he may find interesting and he'd like to meet with him later, after the meeting. "I'm thinking that the meeting should be well done with by midnight and we will have some privacy if we meet in the lunchroom."

Boris said, "I really don't know what you could have that would be of interest to me or why you have to be so secretive, but I'll come."

Leonard took a cup of coffee and sat out on the loading dock with it, thinking that perhaps he was enjoying his last summer night, and not because it was the end of summer.

They assembled back in the lunchroom for the meeting, and Leonard felt the whole thing was a sham and thought maybe Abe should just save everyone a lot of mental gymnastics and just cancel it.

Abe asked them all to please be seated. He and Cille sat next to each other, with Abe at the head of the table. Leonard sat across from Cille. He wanted to be able to see her facial expressions during the meeting. He was happy when Natasha sat down next to Cille. Boris sat at the other end of the table and then Tom came in and sat next to Leonard. He told them that Liv would be there shortly. Morrie was nowhere to be seen and Leonard took this as a good sign—maybe he was doing something in the way of preparing to apprehend Boris and Richard. Richard was not there, as Leonard had expected and when Jill came in last, she said nothing and just sat down next to Tom. There was some more milling around while people decided to get drinks and chat.

Abe called the meeting to order at about quarter after seven, saying he figured the other two would probably show up shortly. "It is a bit disconcerting when we are trying to live as a group, supposedly in harmony to produce a cohesive social unit where we can all benefit to the fullest and use our individual potentials in a coordinated way, and yet some of this cohesive group cannot seem to manage their time well enough to show up on time for group meetings. Be that as it may, I think we should begin. In case anyone didn't know it, this is a fairly diverse group who have chosen to live together in order to accomplish some things that we may not be able to accomplish were we to live separated by space and circumstance. I had a vision for this place and the people who voluntarily formed this association. I saw it as a beginning for an organization, or better yet, an organism, that would transform our immediate environment and become a nexus from which our ideas would spread. As you know, I am a dreamer, but I thought it was possible to bring this dream into the real world.

"After the sudden turn of events that has occurred since Friday, I question this vision. Unfortunately, I cannot ignore that there has been a sudden collapse of the social structure upon which this group was based. An influence has intruded from the outside, and I cannot help but see that that influence has a name and it is none other than Leonardo…"

Leonard felt like he had been hit with a hammer between the eyes. He actually jumped up, and turned toward Abe. A flood of emotions filled him and ran over—he felt his face turn red. As he pointed to himself with a look of total denial, he felt suddenly that he was in some perverse reenactment of the painting "The Last Supper" and he was playing the role of Judas. He looked around the table. Cille looked as shocked as he was, and Natasha was getting out of her chair with a look of horror and anger on her face. He looked again at Abe, thinking that it was a weird joke and Abe would suddenly laugh and end the spell, but Abe was looking at him with Christ-like sorrow in his eyes. He felt Tom next to him, touching him, but looked past him towards Boris who was smiling in triumph--a puppetmaster's smile of one who sees everything falling into place the way he intended.

Lastly he looked at Jill. She has a look of total amazement— of childlike wonderment—almost a grin.

Abe waited for a moment and said, "So, Leo, as long as you are on your feet, I think this is a good time for you to leave. Go. We'll help you get your things packed up and out to your car. I'll even give you money for gas, since you seem to be so concerned about money. Sorry I don't have it in silver."

Leonard felt hot, like he had just entered a sauna. He pushed his chair back as he instinctively tried to get his back against a wall for protection. Cille had moved over and was touching Abe and Natasha had come around the table towards Leonard as

Morrie came into the room, followed by Richard. Their appearance seemed to seal the betrayal. If Morrie and Richard were together, Leonard had no hope. Natasha was talking to him and holding his arm and Tom was on the other side, also touching his arm.

Jill had started to walk toward Leonard, but stopped when Richard entered the room. Jill walked toward Richard, but he ignored her and went over to Boris and whispered something to in his ear. Morrie continued into the room and stood by Liv and whispered something to her.

Abe called them back to the business at hand and quieted them down. Everyone but Leonard and Morrie had taken their seats. Leonard had hardly noticed that Morrie was standing next to him when Abe said, "The two latecomers might be interested to know that I have asked Leonardo to leave our merry group, as he has been a disruptive influence and has violated several of our rules—most notable the rule against having guns." Morrie grabbed Leonard's wrist and twisted his arm behind his back. "Leonardo, would you please give Morrie your gun? The gun you have in your waistband."

This was the ultimate betrayal Leonard thought as he reached under his shirt and took out the little. 22 and handed it to Morrie. Morrie expertly tucked the gun into his own waistband as he released Leonard and stepped away from him.

"Now," continued Abe, "that Leonardo is no longer a danger to himself and others…"

Boris sniggered and Abe smiled benignly.

"Cille has pointed out to me that it would be downright unsociable to throw Leonardo out into the dark of night," Abe continued, "so we will allow him to stay here tonight and have him pack up and leave first thing in the morning."

Leonard numbly walked out of the room. He didn't know what to do or where to go. How could he stay there that night after this? He had misjudged everyone, everything. He felt used, used up, and alone. He went and sat on the fender of his car, trying to make sense of it all, trying to salvage some shred of hope, something to keep him from total despair. "To hell with it all," he said, "I tried to help them…how could I have been so wrong!?" He saw a person's shape on the loading dock in the dim light cast from the windows of the building. He thought, "Go ahead, do your worst, there is no way I can stop you now." He wondered if they had found the other weapons in the kitchen. Probably, they seemed to have known everything.

"Leonardo…" the shadowy figure called to him—it was Natasha.

"What?" he croaked.

"Don't be afraid," she came down the steps, "I don't want to scare you," she said as she walked toward him. She stopped and stood when she was a ways away. "May I talk to you?"

"Sure, talk to me, talk at me, kill me. What does it matter now?"

She came closer. "I disagree with everything Abe said in there—I wanted you to know this. You are not alone."

"Well, I appreciate the thought, really I do…it means a lot. I feel like the bottom has dropped out of my world, but you have given me some small thread to hang onto. But, for your own sake—you have to live with these people—you should forget me and get back in there and protect yourself. If they find you with me, you will be in danger."

"Less danger than you may think," she said.

Leonard wasn't sure how to take that. After all that had happened, he was afraid she'd tell him that she also had lied and had been in cahoots with Boris all along and so was not in danger from him. "Tell me. What just happened in there? Who is Abe really? What is going on? Who are you?"

"For your own good, I cannot give to you answers right now. Trust me."

"Oh, yeah! Trust you—like I trusted Abe, like I trusted Cille! Like I trusted my gut instincts about this whole God forsaken mess! How could I be so stupid!"

"Leonard, trust me! You must just hang on a little longer—do not do anything rash. All I can tell you is it will be okay. I have said too much now." She squeezed his hands and ran back to the building and went inside.

He stood and walked away from the car, thinking that if nothing else, he might be less of a target out of the light of the building. He mulled over what Natasha had just said. *Trust her…trust her about what? About what? It was she who had told him to trust Abe. It was she who had warned him about Boris. And now Abe had totally fucked him over, apparently believing...what? That Boris was harmless? But was any of it true? Had Abe been an agent of a foreign government? Had Boris? How did the rest of them fit in? Was any of it true?*

But then he remembered the papers. He had held them in his hands; had read them. *Could he have misinterpreted them? If Cille was involved, could she have led him to see things in the papers that weren't there? But if the papers weren't what they seemed to be, then none of it was true, none of it mattered, Abe and Boris were not spies, and this whole thing was a mental construct. There were no plots, these were just a bunch of plain folks trying their hand at urban homesteading, just as they appeared. Had his paranoia gotten so out of control as to make him imagine this whole scenario? Was any of it real? Maybe Abe was right. Maybe he was so sick that he was a threat to the stability of this group of people just trying to live together in harmony? Oh, God, what had he done?*

He sensed someone in the darkness nearby. Boris's voice came out of a darker shadow within the shadowy landscape, "Leonardo...having a moment of self doubt? Not so cocky now, are you?"

Leonard didn't answer. Found himself wanting to run, wishing he had a gun. But then he caught himself—this was the very thinking that was always getting him in trouble. Good thing he wasn't armed. He thought that there had been so many times in the past where he had mistaken something harmless as a threat. *Where was a mental health professional when you needed one?*

"Leonardo, don't torture yourself—that's my job. How can I kill thee, let me count the ways!" Boris's voice came to him and Leonard blinked and shook his head. Was he totally losing it? He thought he heard rustling behind him. He walked quickly toward the voice. That should be unexpected in any event.

He ran into someone. "What's your hurry—don't like my company?" Boris said. Now Leonard could see him—he had some helmet or something with goggles on his head. Leonard thought they looked like night vision goggles. Not just anyone would have such things. He had to get to the light, take away Boris's advantage. With a million thoughts flitting and darting like bats seeking moths in the darkness, Leonard realized that the reappearance of Boris in this way meant that Leonard had been right. Unless this was a hallucination. But self preservation was taking precedence and Leonard was backing toward the light. He could plainly see the night vision apparatus and didn't think he could be imagining it. Suddenly he remembered the knife hanging from the lanyard around his neck. He unbuttoned one button on his shirt so he could get at the knife handle more easily.

Boris said, "Is the night so warm...?" He continued speaking, "We will try the non-violent approach one more time, although at this point, I think it safe to say, no one would miss you if you disappeared. Maybe you decided not to wait till morning and just cleared out tonight and good riddance to you. No? But, being the nice guy that I am, I will continue with our first plan..."

Someone left the building and walked noisily across the loading dock, "Leonard, are you out there?"

"Yes, over here!" Leonard called, hoping to end this stalemate in the darkness, certain that Tom or Richard or someone else was waiting out there besides Boris. He felt that could hear them breathing.

Boris stepped in closer and murmured, "We will meet at midnight as planned. Make sure you have the package!" Boris backed away and disappeared into the darkness.

Leonard ran to the loading dock and mounted the steps toward where Cille was, as she started down. He caught up with her and took her inside. "Thank you for being here for me—you may have saved my life," he told her. "Sorry to be so dramatic."

When they got inside, Leonard felt a little safer. But with the safety of the building and away from the darkness, Leonard's doubts returned. "Cille, am I crazy?"

"Not entirely," She gave him a peck on the cheek and said, "Trust in yourself…"

Boris walked through the door and Cille walked past him and left.

Boris said, "Oh, there's something I didn't get a chance to show you outside—come with me, please." Leonard wanted to do anything but go back out into the darkness with Boris. Boris motioned with the flashlight he held—as if the flashlight were a gun and Leonard went back outside. Leonard had pretty good night vision and the flashlight did more to make it harder to see than to help. Fortunately, Boris used it mostly to guide his own steps as he led them down the rocky path to the bottom of the ravine at the edge of the stream. Boris called over his shoulder, "Be careful, there's already been one tragic accident tonight."

Leonard slid down the last steep part of the gravel strewn path and almost fell where Boris shown his flashlight. There in the circle of light, was Morrie, face up, staring blindly into the starry sky. Leonard realized that the stark shadow in the dirt where Morrie's head lay was not just shadow—it was wet with blood.

Boris sighed dramatically. "So, I am afraid there will be no cavalry to the rescue at the end of this movie…" He shown the light in Leonard's face, "Now don't you go getting sick on me— you'll mess up the evidence. Poor guy slipped and fell. The devil only knows what he was doing down here in the dark of night. Obviously slipped and fell. Who knows what he was looking for." Boris pushed the body with his foot and it rolled into the stream and disappeared. "I just wanted to see just how dangerous it can be when you're unsure of your footing. Now the poor man is truly retired!"

Boris reached into a pocket and brought out a gun. "Oh, and I believe this is yours. Morrie certainly has no need of it now."

"What did you do, shoot him with it and now give the gun to me to frame me?"

"Wow, that would be pretty devious. You might make a good operative! But on second thought, you are just too slow."

Leonard put his thumb between the hammer and the firing pin and sniffed the muzzle of the gun—it had been fired. He removed the magazine and dropped it in his pocket, he was surprised that it seemed full. He dropped the gun in another pocket.

Boris said, "I am wondering why you didn't try to shoot me with that gun."

"To be honest, I didn't think it was loaded, or I would have." He thought quickly and added, "Then too, if I'd have shot you, I would get no money. I was thinking that the document you want must be worth a little something. Some token of your appreciation so I could make a fresh start—my thirty pieces of silver."

Boris laughed as he started back up the path. "You Americans, it's always the money. You'd sell your own granny for a buck."

"Well, wasn't it Lenin who said, 'Tell two capitalists you are going to hang them and they'll argue about who sells you the rope,'?"

Boris laughed and continued up the embankment. "I suppose we can give you a little something. See you at midnight." Leonard thought that he could have shot him, and still could shoot him, but he just wasn't sure enough about the gun—plus he had no idea where Richard was, or who else was on Boris's side out there in the darkness with a rifle and night vision scope.

When Leonard got to the top, Boris was gone. Leonard walked back down the path and took out the gun. He wiped the gun with his shirt tail and did the same with the magazine and re-inserted it. "I may regret this," he thought, as he wrapped the gun in a tissue and threw it as far as he could upstream into the river.

He walked back into the building and looked at the clock. It was 10 after 11.

Leonard walked into the lunchroom. It was empty and he went into the adjoining kitchen and found the box untouched. He checked out the guns and made sure they were loaded. He had told Boris to meet him there at midnight. Sort of the antithesis of "high noon." He thought of a samurai he'd read about that showed up at a duel very early. His opponents had thought to show up early and ambush him, but he was already hidden when his opponents showed up. The samurai had darted out from his hiding spot and killed them all. Leonard went back to the lunchroom and flipped the small, square table on its side, so its bottom was facing away from the door and taped the sawed off to it and flipped it back up. He got the folder and put it on the table, then poured himself a cup of coffee and settled in at the table. He took a large knife from a neck strap and placed it, still in its sheath on the table next to the cup of coffee. He made sure the revolver was secure in the small of his back.

At about 11:40, he heard the stairway door open and two sets of footsteps. They paused in the corridor and he heard some muffled voices and one set of footsteps come towards the door to the lunchroom. Through the glass windows facing the corridor, he saw Richard walk up, hesitate, and then walk into the room. Richard saw Leonard and stopped short, then continued in, nonchalantly.

"Ah," Richard said, "I see there's still coffee. Thought I'd get a cup before I went to bed."

"Yup. It's not too burnt tasting," Leonard said, indicating his own cup.

Richard went to the coffee pot and filled a cup with coffee and walked out again. Leonard watched him go past the windows and heard the footsteps fade and then stop. A moment later he heard different footsteps and saw Boris through the window. Leonard put his hands on the coffee cup.

Boris came in and Leonard lifted both hands said, "You just missed Richard—maybe passed him on the stairs."

Boris said nothing and stood at Leonard's table. Then, as if noticing it for the first time, said, "What's the knife for?" He sniggered, "I am reminded of a line from an American movie. You probably didn't know that I learned lots of my English from American movies. So, I tell you, 'Leave it to a wop to bring a knife to a gun fight,'"

"I saw that movie, 'The Untouchables' and it was Sean Connery's character that said it." Leonard placed his left hand on the knife and his other hand in his lap. "You must remember what happened just before that too?"

"Ah, so you have a shotgun hidden in your Victrola?" Boris said with a smile.

"Kind of like that….Since you are a fan of American movies, you may recall a Western with Gregory Peck as a gunman. He's sitting in a bar when another gunslinger comes in and challenges him. Peck tells him, 'How do you know that right now I don't have my gun out under this table?'"

"Yes, I did see that movie—and the other guy backs down and it turns out that Gregory Peck just had a knife and was trimming his nails under the table. What you call 'a bluff,' am I not right?"

Boris's hand came out from under his windbreaker and it held a nasty looking pistol. He said, "But, as I said, you have a knife. Whereas," he jiggled the pistol for emphasis, "I have a gun. And I don't believe you have a revolver under the table. Maybe that pipsqueak. 22."

"Well…"Leonard squeezed the trigger on the shotgun and blew Boris's legs out from under him. "That's where you are wrong. I would never presume to emulate Gregory Peck's acting ability." He crouched down quickly, putting the shotgun under Boris's chin and pulled the second trigger. The eruption of sound, fire, smoke and gore seemed to fill the room. Leonard heard footsteps and pulled the revolver from his waist band and shot Richard in the face as he stopped at the window. "There, now you can live up to your name."

Leonard surveyed the abattoir he had made of the lunch room and said, "Clean up on aisle three!" Then he vomited. He vomited until only bile came up and his stomach muscles ached from clenching.

He heard more footsteps, and found the strength to bring the gun up to cover the hallway.

"Oh, my God!"

Recognizing Jill's voice, Leonard tried to yell, tried to jump up to stop him before he could get to Richard's body. But his voice came out a croak and his legs were too rubbery to hold him up. "I'm afraid I've really killed your turtle now," he croaked and finally got to his feet. It was too late, as he skated through the doorway on a slick of blood and brain matter, Jill was there, holding Richard who was staring at the ceiling, pupils fixed and dilated.

Leonard got the gun up as footsteps pounded on the stairs and Cille ran around the corner into the corridor, followed by Abe. Leonard let his gun hand drop, then tucked the gun back in his waistband. He stopped Cille before she could see the state of the hallway wall or the lunchroom. He shepherded her and Abe back the way they'd come. "It's pretty gruesome back there, you really don't want to see it."

"You bastard! You killed Richard!"

Leonard turned to see Jill holding the gun he had taken out of Richard's hand. Leonard raised his hands. "Jill, he was trying to kill me, I had no choice. Please…"

He felt his own gun being pulled from his waistband and thought, "I'm dead."

Leonard felt a surprising sense of peace, knowing there was nothing to save him now. He watched himself as if he were a balloon floating above his own head, like some Goodyear blimp reporting on the spectacle unfolding below for all the sports fans out there. He heard himself say, "I love you." Saw the hatred drop off of Jill's face and saw her hand drop with the gun; saw the gun drop from her hand and bounce off the floor. All happened in slow motion while he watched himself spin and deflect the hand holding his gun.

The explosion of the gun happened in real time and he was back in his body, Abe's forearm clamped in his hands as he used an Aiki-jutsu move to disarm Abe. The gun clattered to the floor as Abe followed it.

Leonard held Abe in the arm lock, kneeling on his chest, not sure what to do next. Then he heard Cille screaming—and realized she had been screaming for several seconds.

Liv rushed up from somewhere and persuaded Leonard to let Abe up. Liv had a collection of guns, two dangled from her left hand—Richard's and Boris's, Leonard assumed. Her other hand held her ID badge. Liv crouched down and added Leonard's gun to the collection.

Leonard stood up. Everything seemed unnaturally bright and his eyes stung. He felt like he had been freeze dried and at any second was going to disintegrate into dust. He looked at Cille, "'Lucy'" he said, "'You've got a lot of 'splainin' to do!'"

Within seconds, it seemed, the place was crawling with stoical guys and a couple women, in dark suits, all running around with very purposeful expressions. Liv led him in handcuffs out onto the loading dock and let him sit down there. He started to shiver and someone put a blanket over his shoulders, though he figured it was at least 70 degrees out. Abe and Cille and Liv were talking under the light near the doorway. Jill was led, sobbing, to a dark car.

Another blank-faced person stomped up the steps and joined Liv. He and Liv talked for a moment and then Cille and Abe joined in. Soon Liv detached herself from the group and came over to Leonard. She lit a cigarette and offered him one. He stuck it in his mouth with his cuffed hands and she lit it for him. He inhaled deeply, and coughed. "God, I haven't had a cigarette since I was arrested…"

"Yeah, for that pot charge in 1972, when you spent a night in Washtenaw County Jail?" Liv concluded.

"Well, actually it was only two hours, though it seemed like the whole night." He lifted his hands to take the cigarette from his lips and Liv grabbed his hands and removed the cuffs. He thanked her as he exhaled a cloud of smoke. "So, now what?" he asked.

"Abe vouches for you. We have a lot of stuff on tape, some videos—some of which makes you look pretty bad, by the way…"

"I don't photograph well."

"Yeah," Liv took a drag on her own cigarette and blew it out the side of her mouth so it didn't engulf Leonard. "Know anything about Morrie?"

"I'm sorry, but he's dead…I don't know for sure who killed him, Boris or Richard, but he is dead. I'm sorry. Boris showed me the body and then pushed it into the river—it's downstream somewhere. I guess I should tell you one more thing that makes it look bad for me—I think they used my gun, the. 22, to kill him."

"The. 22? Well, everyone saw Morrie take that from you. So you are in the clear there. Do you know where the gun is?"

"I…it's in the river. Umm, aren't you going to Mirandize me—read me my rights?"

"We don't plan on arresting you. Should we?"

"Well, no…but…"

"You did okay for a poor slob that was drawn into this situation without prior knowledge of what is going on. Though, for an innocent person, you seem to know way too much and have way too much familiarity with weapons. Plus, of course possession of a sawed off shotgun would be a Federal offense, just so you know for future reference." She paused and smoked thoughtfully for a minute, "I must say, you are unique…"

"And thank God for that!" laughed Leonard, humorlessly.

"And strangely attractive. I don't mix 'business' and pleasure, but when the smoke has cleared from this godawful hash you made, maybe we could have a cup of coffee, some morning, after a night of wanton sex."

Leonard looked at her. She stubbed out the cigarette, and helped him climb to his feet. She stuck a card in his pocket. "Don't lose that."

He walked back to Abe and Cille. The Fed standing with them said goodbye and walked back down the steps to a car, got in back and the car drove away. He never looked at Leonard.

Abe looked at Leonard. "You are probably wondering what is going on."

Leonard didn't know whether to hug Abe or punch him out, but was so drained he could barely stand and only managed to murmur, "Yeah, I am a bit confused."

"First. Let me apologize for what I put you through! But I wanted to draw Boris out and wanted you out of danger. I knew if I told you anything, there was a possibility of it being overheard, and I also needed your real reaction to what I said. If I had clued you in, I don't think your reaction would have been as genuine."

"That's certainly true—my reaction to what you said was nothing if not genuine. Holy cow, do you have any idea what you put me through! Even now, I am doubting my very sanity. I have no idea, none whatsoever, what is real right now. If leprechauns and Martians started cavorting across this loading dock, it wouldn't phase me in the least. If your face started melting and you started speaking v-e-r-r-y s-l-o-w-l-y in a deep voice or if you suddenly vomited snakes, it wouldn't surprise me at all."

"Leonard, I think you are exaggerating just a bit!"

"Maybe just a smidge…." Leonard held up his thumb and forefinger with a teeny gap between.

"I apologize, for my accusations and how that hurt you, but also for my plan not working to keep you out of danger. But you handled it well; surprisingly well, surpassingly well I would say. Wow. But I see that is a painful subject…sorry."

"You do know that Morrie…what happened to Morrie?" Leonard asked, reluctantly.

"Just that he didn't show up as planned…what happened to Morrie?" Abe asked, concern in his voice.

"I am sorry…he was killed. Boris or Richard shot him with my gun."

Abe sat down on the step. "Oh, my…Are you sure he is dead?"

"Boris made it a point to show me his body—he is dead."

"Where is he?"

"Boris had the body down there, on the river bank. He showed me the body, I guess to assure my compliance, then kicked it into the river. It's probably down stream somewhere. I think the Feds are looking for him—I told Liv."

"It's good that she knows. It must have been a shock to her."

"I suppose so."

Abe heaved a deep sigh, "I guess that explains why he didn't show up to help you with Boris and Richard."

"Yes, he had been dead for at least an hour by then. That's why I went ahead with my plan. Boris himself said there would be no cavalry to the rescue and I wasn't counting on anyone else to help. I figured if they killed Morrie, there was no one to come to my aid. I was more afraid the others would show up and get hurt—like Natasha or Jill. I didn't know whether to trust them, I guess I was trusting Natasha, but I didn't want her to get hurt. Jill was a total puzzle. How is he, by the way?"

"Jill is taking it bad—he is in shock. That was a brilliant strategy, by the way, your telling him you loved him."

"That was no strategy. It just came out. At that moment…I felt that I did love him. It was quite an overpowering feeling. I can't explain it. I must talk to him—I don't want him to think I lied to him, that I said that as a ploy to save my life."

Leonard wanted to sit and do nothing, but knew the lunchroom was a wreck and probably ribboned off as a crime scene. He asked Abe and Cille if there were someplace they could go and talk, as he felt that sleep was out of the question.

"Let's all adjourn to our place," said Abe.

Cille said, "That's fine, but, Leonard, you probably don't know what you look like, but a shower and a new set of clothes would definitely be in order."

"Oh, yeah, I can imagine how I look…" mumbled Leonard.

"Only if you have a very vivid imagination," Cille returned.

"Okay, I'll run up to the roof and take a shower and then come to your place."

"If you don't mind my going through your things, I'll bring you another set of clothes and a towel…." Said Cille

"I think they may want the clothes you are wearing for forensics anyway," Abe interjected.

"Oh, right…." mumbled Leonard—"I suppose someone from the FBI should take them from me—chain of evidence and all that…."

"I'll get an agent up to the roof to take them from you," said Abe.

Abe left and Leonard and Cille went up the stairs, Cille stopping at his floor to get his things. Leonard said he needed a hug, but could wait till after he was cleaned up. Cille set the lantern down and disappeared.

There was a mirror near the shower, but Leonard passed it without looking into it. He waited, and started to sit down in the lawn chair someone had brought up there, but decided not to get blood on it. He stood for a while and was so weak that he sat down in the chair anyway. Cille came over and Liv was with her. That reminded him of the card Liv had stuck in his pocket. When Liv came close he asked her to get it and put it into his wallet. As he didn't want to get blood on it from his hands. She smiled and deftly removed both the wallet and the card and did as he had asked and put the wallet into the pants that Cille had brought.

Liv told him to undress and held out a plastic bag and he put his socks and shoes, shirt and pants into it and she sealed it. "Underwear too," Liv said.

"Oh," said Leonard and he took off his underpants and held them out, expecting her to bag them to.

She smile mischievously and dropped them on the roof, "Actually, we don't need those for evidence, I just had to see you naked."

Normally this would have excited Leonard, but he just nodded numbly and turned and went into the shower.

"I'll see you at Abe and Cille's when you're done," Liv called to him, "I want to be present for the debriefing, as Abe called it."

Leonard couldn't believe how much blood washed down the drain as he showered. He had to work hard to get it out of his hair and out from under his fingernails. He could imagine he smelled it but when his stomach turned over, he thought of something else. He thought it would have been easier to just shave his head the way Boris did, because of how the blood had matted his hair. He wanted to melt and flow down the drain with the blood and water. He wanted total oblivion. Soon the water was becoming cold and he figured he'd have to settle for as clean as he was then and turned the water off and got out of the shower enclosure.

Cille was there and held out the towel and he took it and dried himself. He was feeling cold again and was glad to get some fresh clothes on. He remembered the assignations he'd had in the shower with Natasha and asked about her.

Cille shook her head and said she hadn't seen her. "Let's go downstairs…"

Leonard walked down to their flat with Cille, stopping at the doorway to hug her. He said, "You don't appreciate people until you know how quickly they can be taken away."

He walked in. Abe was there and Cille sat in a chair next to him. He was relieved to see Natasha sitting on the couch and Liv was sitting casually on the arm of the same couch. Leonard couldn't resist, "You're probably wondering why I called you all together here…" He laughed, but no one else seemed to catch the humor. He tried again, "Surprise!" and threw his hands in the air, "Oh, my birthday! You shouldn't have!" That brought a couple smiles and a chuckle. For his last attempt he said, "I'm parched, anyone got anythin' to drink?" He was surprised when Natasha stood up and poured him a tumbler of whiskey and brought it and the bottle over to him.

"I am so glad to see you!" he said, giving her a big hug, almost causing her to spill the drink.

She kissed his cheek, "I too am glad to see you. And you are unharmed?"

He took the drink and gulped it down greedily. "Totally unharmed physically. And mentally, who could tell?" He grabbed the bottle and refilled his glass. He noticed how quiet it had gotten as Natasha crossed the room and sat down again. "What about Jill?" Leonard asked, "How's he doing?"

Abe cleared his throat, "He is taking it hard—the loss of Richard. He has been hospitalized for observation and has been sedated." He seemed to notice Leonard's expression and added, "I think it was more because he couldn't face coming back here and he had no place else to go."

"Okay. I'd like to go see him in the morning, maybe someone could show me how to get there," Leonard said.

Natasha raised her hand and said she'd like to do that.

Leonard wanted to chug his second drink, but reluctantly sipped it, thinking it best, perhaps, to remain conscious for the impromptu meeting. He still had a feeling that at any second the bottom could fall out, or the roof cave in, or everything would just disintegrate. "Fuck it," he said out loud and gulped about half of his drink. "As my colleague at Port City Metro used to say, 'I go through life like a dog; if you can't eat it or fuck it, piss on it!'" Smiling grimly, he said, "Here's to mental health week!" and drained the glass. Unsteadily, he poured another glass and slopped it over the edge. "Oops, can't waste this golden elixir of life, *Uh-ska-ba.*"

Liv walked over and stood in front of him. "Don't make me slap you!"

"You know, I almost think…" Leonard was going to say he might like that, but noticing the no nonsense look on her face, said "On second thought, 'Thanks, I don't need that.' Though," he just had to add, "'a slap from you would be like the kiss of an angel.'"

"Don't bet on it!" Liv said, and returned to her place.

Abe cleared his throat again, "I just felt that we needed to talk and wind down. I don't think any of us will be able to sleep any time soon. And," he choked back something, "I just want to start by toasting fallen comrades—Here's to Morris Taylor." He lifted his glass and everyone drank to Morrie.

Leonard bowed his head down and then raised it and said, "I know this is pitifully feeble after all that's happened, but, I am sorry."

Cille said, "I think we would all agree that we would have preferred events to have transpired in a different way than they did, and we are all sorry they didn't, but what happened happened. Things could have happened differently, and I although I can see where things could possibly have been better, they could have also been much worse. *Much* worse." She looked at Leonard for a moment, "And Leonard, I am sorry too. I am sorry for bringing you into this, and I am truly sorry for the toll it took on you, but that said, I just cannot imagine a good outcome from all of this without you being here. Sometimes the Universe just seems to pick one person to hinge everything on, and that person in this case, was you. You carried a lot of weight and could have been crushed by that, but you weren't, and I think you have it in you to go on....And I hope that you would stay here with us, you are certainly welcome."

Discussion followed.

CPSIA information can be obtained at www.ICGtesting.com
Printed in the USA
BVOW07s1525270114

343141BV00001B/177/P